STORIES OF THAT TIME

John Wirth

authorHOUSE®

AuthorHouse™
1663 Liberty Drive
Bloomington, IN 47403
www.authorhouse.com
Phone: 1 (800) 839-8640

Published by AuthorHouse 02/15/2016

ISBN: 978-1-5049-7111-9 (sc)
ISBN: 978-1-5049-7112-6 (e)

Print information available on the last page.

This book is printed on acid-free paper.

Cover photo by Oliver Atkins.
Provided by the Richard Nixon Presidential Library and Museum.

ACKNOWLEDGEMENTS

I thank Jon Fletcher of the Nixon Library and Museum for helping me—with exemplary efficiency—choose and obtain the cover photo.

And I thank Mike Collins, Rhea Nolan, Richelle Keith and Nathan Reed, my handlers at AuthorHouse, for their contributions to the prompt actualization of the book.

NOTE

Some persons and events in these stories are (or rather were) "real"—insofar as this term can be applied to matters appearing in the newspaper. Other persons and events, not so much. Others, not at all. I leave it to the reader to guess which is which.

CONTENTS

ONE

The Mangoes 3

A Do 5

TWO

The First Bullfighter of Spain 19

The Safari 21

THREE

Dignity 37

The King and His Court 39

FOUR

Politics 53

The Renegade 55

FIVE

The Russians 71

General G. 74

SIX

The Atheist 87

The Modern Artist 91

SEVEN

The Sweater 109

The Pornographer 112

EIGHT

Violet And Daisy 121
White Sand 123

NINE

The Actress 145
Scene 146

TEN

A Very Queer Thing 163
The Security Advisor 164

ELEVEN

The Attack 187
A Very Splendid Victory 188

TWELVE

The Weapon 195
The Under Secretary 197

THIRTEEN

The Correspondents 223
At the War 225

FOURTEEN

At the Ranch 257
Back at The Ranch 259

About the Author 265

ONE

THE MANGOES

Chairman Mao conveyed his commendations. Chairman Mao commended a worker-peasant propaganda team. The worker-peasant propaganda team had worked at Tsinghua University in Peking. The propaganda team had resolved ideological contradictions between factions of Red Guards. Chairman Mao conveyed his highest commendations. Chairman Mao presented the worker-peasant propaganda team with two mangoes.

The mangoes were enshrined with a portrait of Chairman Mao on an altar at the Peking airport. The mangoes were the chief attraction of the Peking airport. A foreigner leaving Peking had happened to give the mangoes to Chairman Mao. Chairman Mao conveyed the highest commendations of the entire Communist Party along with the mangoes. Two militiamen stood guard in front of the mangoes. The militiamen stood stiffly erect and with one hand held small red books of Chairman Mao's quotations to their breasts. One mango was in a bottle of formaldehyde. In the formaldehyde the mango began to look dark and mushy.

Chairman Mao's presentation of the mangoes to the worker-peasant team was hailed throughout the country. Mass meetings were held in towns and cities to hail Chairman Mao's presentation. Officials declared that Chairman Mao's presentation of the mangoes was very significant. Newspaper editorials interpreted the significance of Chairman Mao's presentation of the mangoes.

Newspaper editorials declared that Chairman Mao's presentation of the mangoes to the worker-peasant propaganda team at Tsinghua University, the base of militant Red Guard factions, demonstrated that

3

the Red Guards were to subordinate themselves to the workers and peasants. The newspaper editorials declared this to be the lesson of Chairman Mao's presentation of mangoes. There was a lesson in every thought and action of Chairman Mao.

An editorial in Jen-Min Jih-Pao commemorated the presentation of the mangoes and the second anniversary of the review by Chairman Mao on August 18, 1966 of hundreds of thousands of Red Guards in Peking.

"For longer than two years the Red Guards have played a vanguard role in attacking revisionists, imperialists and exploiters in pursuing Chairman Mao's Great Proletarian Cultural Revolution," the editorial said.

"The hallmark today of revolutionary spirit in a young person is whether or not he is willing to integrate himself with the broad masses of workers, peasants and soldiers, and does so in practice.

"The laboring masses, the workers and peasants, are the most reliable and resolute revolutionary group and together with the army are the main force.

"Ours is a state of the dictatorship of the proletariat and it does not need intellectuals who look down on the workers and peasants.

"Therefore the Red Guards and all educated young people should make the workers their teachers, steadily reform themselves in the course of long class struggle, earnestly accept the leadership of the working class and conscientiously study Mao Tse-tung's thought, the world outlook of the working class," the editorial said.

The second mango on the altar at the Peking airport was better preserved. The second mango was enshrined in a glass case. A red ribbon was tied around the mango. The ribbon had a bow knot in it.

A DO

They marched up East Sixty-Fifth Street. They marched up East Sixty-Fifth Street towards Park Avenue. Onlookers watched them march up East Sixty-Fifth Street towards Park Avenue. Onlookers asked what it was they were doing as they marched up Sixty-Fifth Street. The onlookers were puzzled. The onlookers could not decide what it was they were doing as they marched up Sixty-Fifth Street. One hundred and thirty of them marched in a file up East Sixty-Fifth Street.

"It's a protest," said an onlooker.

"They're having a love-in," said an onlooker.

"It looks like a graduation procession," said an onlooker.

"It looks like a Shriner's convention," said an onlooker.

They marched out of the Architectural League building and up East Sixty-Fifth Street. They marched out of the Architectural League building at 41 East Sixty-Fifth Street towards Park Avenue. They marched on East Sixty-Fifth Street draped in red acetate cloth. All of them marched draped in the same piece of red acetate cloth. All of them marched draped in a long strip of red acetate cloth. Their heads protruded from holes in the red acetate cloth. There were holes at three-foot intervals along the length of the strip of red acetate cloth. Onlookers asked why they were marching draped in the red acetate cloth. Onlookers asked why all of them were marching draped in the same piece of red acetate cloth. A tuba quintet played as they marched out of the Architectural League building. The name of the tuba quintet was The Solid Foundation. The Solid Foundation tuba quintet played the E-Flat Fugue of Bach as they marched out of the Architectural League building and up East Sixty-Fifth Street towards Park Avenue. Esther Goldstone played the flute as they marched out of the Architectural League building. Esther Goldstone was a flutist. Esther Goldstone played the E-Flat Fugue of Bach with The Solid Foundation tuba quintet. Esther Goldstone played the flute on the balcony of the Architectural League building as they marched out of the Architectural League building and up East Sixty-Fifth Street.

John Lee Bryant marched up East Sixty-Fifth Street towards Park Avenue. John Lee Bryant wore a black Navajo hat. John Lee Bryant's hair was black. John Lee Bryant's black hair was long. John Lee Bryant's black hair reached to his shoulders.

"It's probably the world's biggest dress," said John Lee Bryant.

"We're going around the block," said John Lee Bryant.

"This was my idea," said John Lee Bryant.

"Call the parade what you wish. I'm tired of words like 'event' and 'happening' with their open-ended definitions. I simply call this one a a 'do,' " said John Lee Bryant.

John Lee Bryant was from Detroit. John Lee Bryant was an artist. John Lee Bryant wore a pink silk pants suit. The pink silk pants suit tied at the chin.

"The suit can expand to include five persons if you wish," said John Lee Bryant.

A blonde model marched up East Sixty-Fifth Street. A blonde model marched up East Sixty-Fifth Street draped in red acetate cloth. The blonde model led them up East Sixty-Fifth Street. The blonde model was a friend of John Lee Bryant. The blonde model's name was Electra Impulse. The blonde model wore only a blouse under the red acetate cloth. The blonde model took off the blouse.

"It's delightful to feel the wind," said the blonde model.

Edward Fleck marched up East Sixty-Fifth Street. Edward Fleck was a student. Edward Fleck was a student at Columbia University. Edward Fleck marched draped in red acetate cloth up East Sixty-Fifth Street. Edward Fleck marched backwards.

"Why not? It's releasing," said Edward Fleck.

Edward Fleck talked with Shirley Liedermann. Shirley Liedermann marched draped in red acetate cloth up East Sixty-Fifth Street. Shirley Liedermann marched up East Sixty-Fifth Street behind Edward Fleck. Shirley Liedermann was an administrative aide. Shirley Liedermann was an administrative aide at the Cornell University College of Architecture.

"It's nice to be able to *say* something to a person for once," said Shirley Liedermann,

Peter Eberhardt marched draped in red acetate cloth. Peter Eberhardt marched up Sixty-Fifth Street. Peter Eberhardt's father and mother marched up East Sixty-Fifth Street. Peter Eberhardt was four years old. Peter Eberhardt's head protruded from a hole in the strip of red acetate cloth. Peter Eberhardt withdrew his head from the hole in the strip of red acetate cloth. Peter Eberhardt threw off the strip of red acetate cloth. Under the strip of red acetate cloth Peter Eberhardt ran to others under the strip of red acetate cloth. Peter Eberhardt tickled their legs.

Robert Lester marched up East Sixty-Fifth Street. Robert Lester was from Tennessee, Robert Lester was an architect.

"I feel slightly silly, but it's a lot of fun. I feel kind of young. It's like the first time I was taken to the fair. You don't know what to expect. There's a lot of color and a bit of confusion," said Robert Lester.

They marched draped in the strip of red acetate cloth up East Sixty-Fifth Street. They marched in a file up East Sixty-Fifth Street. Some of them who had been marching in the front of the file withdrew their heads from holes in the red acetate cloth. Some of them who had been marching in the front of the file ran near the rear of the file. Some of them who had been marching at the head of the file marched draped in the red acetate cloth near the rear of the file.

"We can't have any gaps in the holes," said a man who had been marching at the head of the file who marched near the rear of the file. They marched up East Sixty-Fifth Street to Park Avenue. They marched from East Sixty-Fifth Street onto Park Avenue. They marched on Park Avenue. They marched north on Park Avenue.

Policemen conducted them from East Sixty-Fifth Street onto Park Avenue. A policeman stood on the corner of East Sixty-Fifth Street and Park Avenue. The policeman looked at them marching from East Sixty-Fifth Street onto Park Avenue. The policeman was puzzled. The policeman could not decide what it was they were doing as they marched onto Park Avenue. An onlooker spoke to the policeman. The onlooker was puzzled.

"Hey, what are they demonstrating against?" said the onlooker.

"I don't figure it," said the onlooker.

They marched north on Park Avenue draped in the red acetate cloth. Onlookers asked what it was they were doing as they marched on Park Avenue. A doorman of the building at 630 Park Avenue was puzzled. The doorman of the building at 630 Park Avenue asked what it was they were doing as they marched past the building at 630 Park Avenue.

"It's for fun?" said the doorman at 630 Park Avenue.

"What're they advertising?" said the doorman at 630 Park Avenue.

They marched from Park Avenue onto East Sixty-Sixth Street. They marched west on East Sixty-Sixth Street. They marched in a file on East Sixty-Sixth Street. Onlookers on East Sixty-Sixth Street were puzzled. They marched onto Madison Avenue from East Sixty-Sixth Street. They marched onto Madison Avenue from East Sixty-Sixth Street draped in red acetate cloth. Onlookers on Madison Avenue could not decide what it was they were doing as they marched on Madison Avenue. Eric Byrnes marched on Madison Avenue. Eric Byrnes marched on Madison Avenue draped in red acetate cloth. Eric Byrnes was a student at Columbia University. "We're Klan members," said Eric Byrnes to an onlooker. "We're having an adventure in communication," said Eric Byrnes to an onlooker.

They marched draped in the strip of red acetate cloth along Madison Avenue. John Lee Bryant cut the strip of red acetate cloth at intervals along the length of the strip of red acetate cloth. John Lee Bryant cut the strip of red acetate cloth after every fifth one of them. They marched in files and columns on Madison Avenue draped in strips of red acetate cloth.

"You see how different it is to interact with only four people," said John Lee Bryant.

They marched into the Architectural League building on East Sixty-Fifth Street. Onlookers near the Architectural League building asked what it was they were doing as they marched into the Architectural League building. The onlookers could not decide what it was they were doing as they marched into the Architectural League building. The onlookers were puzzled. They marched into the banquet room of the Architectural League building. They marched into the banquet room draped in strips of red acetate cloth. John Lee Bryant cut the strips of red acetate cloth at intervals along the lengths of the strip of red acetate cloth. John Lee Bryant cut the strips of red acetate cloth between each of them or between every two of them.

"Now everyone should be able to work on interpersonal relations," said John Lee Bryant.

"You can take off the robes when you feel completely frank," said John Lee Bryant.

"We're having a cocktail party," said John Lee Bryant.

"I thought it was very beautiful, very successful," said John Lee Bryant.

"It's to celebrate the opening of something I call 'Mr. Bryant and Six Plays.' That's what I call a series of audience-participation events I've created for the League. It'll run through the third of October. We're going to deal with inter-group and interpersonal communications and behavior. Tomorrow I'll be holding a session all day to discuss what we'll do tomorrow night with the people who'll be participating and anyone else who would like to come.

"For instance, I call one of the plays 'A Hundred in an Airplane.' I'll ask for a hundred volunteers to pretend to fly a hundred-foot-square silk airplane. We'll also do 'Twelve in a Pink Pants.' There'll be twelve people wearing s continuous silk suit and discussing their lifestyles. Then we'll have 'Con-struction of a Mile-Long Strip.' A Chinese tailor is going to sew a mile of acetate into one strip.

"I want people to describe and discuss their perceptions, to become aware of their lifestyles—what they eat, their behavior cycles, everything involved with the way they live. I want people to learn to perceive and relate to the lifestyles of others in order to become really congruent with other people. This is the only way to radically increase the quantity and effectiveness of love in the world.

"I ask the people participating and the audience questions they can discuss to get some insight into these problems. I ask them question like 'What is the speed of an idea?' 'What does pretend mean?' 'Are all people interchangeable at some level?' " said John Lee Bryant.

They stood in the banquet room of the Architectural League building. They threw off strips of red acetate cloth. They drank cocktails standing in the banquet room. They talked standing in the banquet room. They sat on the floor of the banquet room. They sat on the floor of the banquet room drinking cocktails. They sat and lay on the floor of the banquet room drinking cocktails.

"I want everybody to see if he can't direct the channels of inter-perception towards another person and establish a close interrelationship," said John Lee Bryant.

They sat and lay on the floor drinking cocktails and talking. They held hands and embraced on the floor. They held hands and embraced drinking cocktails on the floor. John Lee Bryant sat on the floor of the banquet room drinking cocktails.

"I feel relationships structuring," said John Lee Bryant.

John Lee Bryant sat on the floor of the banquet room drinking cocktails holding hands with a tall girl. John Lee Bryant talked to the tall girl and held hands with the tall girl and drank cocktails on the floor of the banquet room. The blonde model sat on the floor. The blonde model sat on the floor drinking cocktails. The blonde model drank cocktails and embraced a short man. The blonde model drank cocktails and talked to the short man. The short man sat on the floor and drank cocktails and embraced the blonde model on the floor.

John Lee Bryant watched the short man sitting on the floor drink cocktails and embrace the blonde model on the floor. John Lee Bryant watched the blonde model embrace the short man and drink cocktails on the floor. John Lee Bryant stood up on the floor of the banquet room. John Lee Bryant walked on the floor of the banquet room. John Lee Bryant walked on the floor of the banquet room towards the blonde model and the short man drinking cocktails on the floor of the banquet room. John Lee Bryant walked to the blonde model and the short man. The blonde model and the short man drank cocktails and embraced. John Lee Bryant took the hand of the blonde model on the floor. The short man embraced the blonde model.

"Do you mind?" said John Lee Bryant to the short man on the floor.

"I'd like to try and reach out to this girl now. We're close friends," said John Lee Bryant to the short man on the floor.

The short man on the floor embraced the blonde model. The short man on the floor drank cocktails on the floor and embraced the blonde model. John Lee Bryant watched the short man drink cocktails and embrace the blonde model. John Lee Bryant shook his head at the short man on the floor drinking cocktails and embracing the blonde model.

"You might let go of her," said John Lee Bryant to the short man on the floor.

"There's a tall girl over there," said John Lee Bryant to the short man on the floor.

The short man on the floor embraced the blonde model and drank cocktails. The short man embraced the blonde model on the floor of the banquet room. John Lee Bryant watched the short man embrace the blonde model on the floor of the banquet room. John Lee Bryant shook his head at the short man.

"What kind of uniform is he wearing," said a man to John Lee Bryant.

"I don't know why he doesn't answer me," said John Lee Bryant.

"He acts as if he's deaf," said John Lee Bryant.

"I think it would be better if you answered me," said John Lee Bryant to the short man on the floor.

"He's drunk out of his mind. He doesn't hear you," said a man to John Lee Bryant.

"He's a policeman," said a man to John Lee Bryant.

"He's no policeman," said a man to John Lee Bryant.

"If you don't mind," said John Lee Bryant to the short man on the floor. The short man embraced the blonde model on the floor. The short man drank cocktails on the floor. John Lee Bryant looked at the short man embrace the blonde model on the floor.

"Come on over there with me," said John Lee Bryant to the blonde model.

"Who is he? I've never seen him before," said John Lee Bryant.

"He's in the army," said a man to John Lee Bryant.

"Who told you about coming here?" said John Lee Bryant to the short man on the floor.

"He's not in the army," said a man to John Lee Bryant.

"I didn't see him march with us," a man said to John Lee Bryant.

"He didn't march with us," said a man to John Lee Bryant.

"Does anyone know who he is?" said John Lee Bryant.

"Look. He's a messenger from Western Union," said a man to John Lee Bryant.

"I guess he *is* a messenger from Western Union," said John Lee Bryant.

"What are you doing here?" said John Lee Bryant to the short man on the floor.

The short man sat on the floor. The short man drank cocktails on the floor. The short man embraced the blonde model on the floor. The short man embraced the blonde model on the floor of the banquet room of the Architectural

League building. The short man pulled several papers from his pocket and dropped them on the floor.

"They're telegrams," said a man to John Lee Bryant.

"He's too drunk to deliver them. Maybe we should call the company and have them come and get him," said a man to John Lee Bryant.

"One of these is for you," said a man to John Lee Bryant.

A man handed John Lee Bryant a telegram. John Lee Bryant opened the telegram. John Lee Bryant read the telegram. The short man embraced the blonde model on the floor. The short man drank cocktails on the floor.

"My God. Bad news. What do you think of that? My mother died," said John Lee Bryant.

"And this fellow's been here for an hour with this and he hasn't given it to me," said John Lee Bryant.

John Lee Bryant seized the short man on the floor. John Lee Bryant swore at the short man on the floor. John Lee Bryant dragged the short man across the floor. John Lee Bryant dragged the short man across the floor of the banquet room. John Lee Bryant dragged the short man out of the banquet room. John Lee Bryant dragged the short man to the door of the Architectural League building. John Lee Bryant pushed the short man out the door of the Architectural League building. John Lee Bryant shouted at the short man and pushed the short man out the door of the Architectural League building.

They sat and lay on the floor of the banquet room of the Architectural League building. They drank cocktails sitting and lying on the floor of the banquet room. They embraced and held hands talking and drinking cocktails on the floor of the banquet room. John Lee Bryant sat on the floor of the banquet room. John Lee Bryant sat drinking cocktails on the floor of the banquet room. On the floor of the banquet room they extended their sympathies to John Lee Bryant upon the death of his mother. On the floor of the banquet room John Lee Bryant thanked them for extending their sympathies upon the death of his mother. They sat and lay embracing and holding hands and talking and drinking cocktails on the floor of the banquet room of the Architectural League building on East Sixty-Fifth Street.

"I don't know how the telegram company can expect to do business if it employs jokers like that," said John Lee Bryant.

TWO

THE FIRST BULLFIGHTER
OF SPAIN

On Saturday at Almeria the bullfighter was shouted out of the ring. The bullfighter waved his cape at the bull. The bull became angry. The bull attacked the cape. The cape was torn. The bullfighter attempted to kill the bull. The bullfighter attempted to kill the bull a great many times. It was a strong bull. It was a stubborn bull. The bull stubbornly refused to be killed. The bullfighter attempted to kill the bull again. The bull refused to be killed. The bullfighter pouted at the bull. The bull bellowed. The officials of the bullfight ordered the bull to be led away for slaughter. The spectators shouted. The bullfighter smiled and bowed elaborately at the spectators.

He was Manuel Benitez, El Cordobés, the highest-paid matador in Spain. On Sunday in Marbella he refused to fight the bull. He complained the bull was too dangerous to fight. He complained the bull had fought before. He complained the bull had learned the tricks of matadors. It would be very dangerous to fight the bull. Very possibly he would be killed. The bull refused to charge the horses of the picadores to be speared. Several times the bull charged the banderilleros and the two motion picture photographers. The banderilleros thrust extraordinarily long banderillas into the bull's back to punish the bull. He attempted to make passes with the bull. The bull charged him and refused to follow his cape. He swore at the bull and spit at it. The bull charged him. He stepped out of the way of the bull rapidly. He sighed. He shook his head grimly.

He walked towards the presidential box and loudly refused to fight the bull. He was fined seventy-two dollars for disrespect to the officials of the bullfight. The officials ordered the bull to be led away. The officials fined the owners of the bull one hundred forty-four dollars. The officials agreed that the bull had fought before. The spectators cheered him for refusing to fight the bull. Another bull was led into the bullring. He fought the bull. The bull followed his cape. The spectators cheered. He killed the bull. The spectators cheered. The spectators awarded him the ears and tail of the bull. All the spectators agreed that he had fought the bull very brilliantly and bravely.

THE SAFARI

"Maybe we shouldn't go after all. Maybe it's too dangerous," said the elderly gentleman.

"It's not too dangerous for you," said the young woman.

The young woman smiled at the elderly gentleman. The young woman embraced the elderly gentleman. The young woman kissed the ear of the elderly gentleman.

The elderly gentleman adjusted the belts of his safari jacket. There were many belts on his safari jacket. The elderly gentleman inspected the leather patches of his safari jacket. There were many leather patches on his safari jacket.

"I don't suppose two hundred dollars is too much to pay for a jacket. They're supposed to be the best outfitters in Nairobi," said the elderly gentleman.

"The jacket is very lovely. You look very nice," said the young woman.

"I don't know. Look at the statement they're making us sign. It says 'I undertake the impending expedition with the understanding that neither the Aberdare National Park nor Kenya Hotels Limited or any of its employees are to be held responsible for any personal injury or loss that I may suffer from any cause whatsoever, including the wrongful act or omission of any person employed by the company.' That sounds like it might be pretty dangerous," said the elderly gentleman.

"You're so brave. I've never made love in the treetops," said the young woman.

"It says we get our money back if we don't come across any elephants or rhinoceroses or buffalo. I was never much of one with animals," said the elderly gentleman.

"You're sweet," said the young women.

The young woman kissed the cheek of the elderly gentleman. The young woman hung on the arm of the elderly gentleman.

"I saw Tyrone Power in that movie by Ernest Hemingway. Where is Mount Kilimanjaro from here, anyway? At least they don't use a truck," said the elderly gentleman.

"Kiss me," said the young woman.

The elderly gentleman kissed the young woman. The young woman kissed the nose of the elderly gentleman. The young woman put her finger in the ear of the elderly gentleman.

"I guess a hundred dollars for one day isn't too much," said the elderly gentleman.

"You're so generous," said the young woman.

"Well, it should be exciting, anyway," said the elderly gentleman.

"You are very brave," said the young woman.

The young woman and the elderly gentleman walked from the Outspan Hotel to the bus. The other tourists walked from the Outspan Hotel to the bus. The tall man stood in the bus. The tall man wore a bush jacket, khaki shorts and white knee socks. The tall man carried a rifle slung over his shoulder.

"I'm sure that man's the white hunter. He looks like an expert. I'm sure nothing could happen to us with him in charge," said the young woman.

"I don't know," said the elderly gentleman.

"You're so adorable," said the young woman.

The young woman smiled at the elderly gentleman. The young woman kissed the elderly gentleman's chin.

The tall man addressed the tourists in the bus.

"Perhaps I should explain that I am the leader of your expedition and also the manager of the hotel. The name's Haynes-Newington, Colonel Edward Haynes-Newington. I don't know if you're interested in history especially but I've been with the army in India and led a brigade in Burma and been a staff police officer here during the Mau Mau affair. Our destination is approximately a hundred miles north of Nairobi, twenty-five miles from here, roughly. An hour, ninety minutes. I should advise you to hang rather firmly onto your seats as the road is none of the best," said the tall man.

The young woman and the elderly gentleman rode in the bus. The bus bounced. The young woman and the elderly gentleman bounced. The elderly gentleman held firmly onto his seat.

"It is pretty rough going out here. Maybe we shouldn't have come," said the elderly gentleman.

"I know nothing really bothers you," said the young woman.

"I guess an elephant could turn this bus over if it really wanted to," said the elderly gentleman.

"You're such a handsome man. I suppose you know you're handsome," said the young woman.

The bus bounced. The young woman and the elderly gentleman bounced.

The bus halted. The tall man stood in the bus. The tall man addressed the tourists in the bus.

"You see by the sign that we are presently twenty-four and a half miles south of the equator and at an elevation of six thousand four hundred and fifty feet. The hotel is two hundred yards from us on that tack behind the stand of bush there. Of course we daren't approach nearer the pond with the bus for fear of putting off the animals. It's my job now to get you to the treehouse in one piece. I should warn you that while I don't consider this little journey especially dangerous nevertheless there does exist the possibility of a person's being run down by an elephant or a buffalo or a rhino at any time. At the approach of animals you will quickly take refuge in one of the hides distributed along the route of march. Of course in the event of emergency I have the gun here," said the tall man.

"Maybe we should have stayed at the hotel," said the elderly gentleman.

"You're such a sport," said the young woman.

The young woman and the elderly gentleman walked through the grass. The other tourists walked through the grass. There was grass along the path to the hotel.

"Are those what they call hides? I don't know if I could get over to one in time if an elephant charged me," said the elderly gentleman.

"I'm sure you could," said the young woman.

"They look like those toilets they have on the streets in Paris," said the elderly gentleman.

"I feel very safe with you," said the young woman.

"I don't see any big animals around," said the elderly gentleman.

"I think I just saw a rabbit," said the young woman.

The young woman and the elderly gentleman climbed the ladder. The other tourists climbed the ladder. There was a ladder up to the hotel.

The tall man addressed the tourists in the bar of the hotel.

"I should assure you that you need have absolutely no fear as to the integrity of this structure. As you saw in coming up the hotel is supported thirty feet off the ground by quite substantial cedar poles. No part of any of the three stories of the hotel is supported by the surrounding trees. In the event of a lightning storm, however, I must ask you all to collect on the lower story near the exits as a precaution against fire. As it happens lightning seems to strike us rather often though as yet without occasioning damage to speak of. Of course smoking is extremely hazardous and is strictly prohibited," said the tall man.

"I think we should have stayed in Nairobi," said the elderly gentleman.

"It's very exciting," said the young woman.

The young woman pressed the hand of the elderly gentleman. The young women winked at the elderly gentleman.

The tourists looked at the baboon sitting on the branch of the tree. The tourists looked at the baboon through the window of the bar. A baboon sat on the branch of a tree.

"I must warn you especially against the baboons that are everywhere in these trees. They have a rather nasty habit of snatching up your film and stringing it out. In fact they'll snatch up about anything. I advise you to keep your windows tightly locked and your zippered things zippered up. We've been compelled a good many times to send the houseboys chasing into the woods after baboons till they drop the passports they've picked up," said the tall man.

"That monkey looks like he could be vicious," said the elderly gentleman.

"He is kind of frightening," said the young woman.

The young woman and the elderly gentleman and the tall man sat on a porch. The young woman and the elderly gentleman and the tall man looked at the watering hole. There was a watering hole near the hotel. The young woman put her arm around the waist of the elderly gentleman. The young woman put her head on the shoulder of the elderly gentleman.

"Animals attracted by the high salt content of the water, you see. We add a bit of salt to make it sure they show," said the tall man.

"There's something drinking there. What's that?" said the elderly gentleman.

"Water hog. Over there. A waterbuck," said the tall man.

"I suppose it's nice to see the animals in spite of the danger," said the elderly gentleman.

"George isn't afraid of any of the animals," said the young woman.

"There isn't any reason to be afraid of them," said the elderly gentleman.

"George's done a lot of dangerous things," said the young woman.

"We're going to be married as soon as they finalize my divorce. I'll be giving my present wife about two million," said the elderly gentleman.

"We serve all sorts here, you know. Of course it's a good deal more democratic than it was. Princess, roadsweeper, we treat them the same. Accommodations same for everybody, maybe a drink on the house or a room with a little better view for certain guests, but every room with the barracks beds, pitcher of water and a few hooks to hang your clothes. Absolutely no one permitted to bring any clothes but the change on his back and night attire. The old Treetops, you had to be a bit of an aristocrat to get in. It was a small place, you see, burned by the Mau Mau in fifty-four. Built in a fig tree with room for just a few couples by Major Eric Sherbrooke Walker in thirty-two. He and Lady Beattie used to entertain all the high mucks, Mountbattens, the Duchess of Kent who just died. Of course our reputation was made when Elizabeth and the Prince stayed the night the King died. That was February fifth, fifty-two. Happened to be in the Queen's escort. She was absolutely magnificent when she heard the news in the morning. Said good-by to the entourage, very friendly, very natural, greeted the airplane crew and flew back to England. She'd been very well trained to be Queen and she acted very finely. Major Walker decided to build a place a bit more elaborate. We sleep forty-three, forty-four with a man on the dining room table. Never close and take in about five thousand a year. We have to limit everyone to a day at a time to accommodate demand. I don't know who all we've had. Last year after the coronation of the Shah of Iran we had Fatemah Pahlavi, his sister, and Leila Hoveyda, the wife of the Prime Minister.

"The last months we've had Prime Minister Tage Erlander of Sweden and President Banda of Malawi, ministers from Yugoslavia, Austria, Germany, the Chief Justice of the Camaroons, a Rockefeller, I don't remember which one. In sixty-six Senator Kennedy came up after his tour about Africa; there were television cameramen all over the place. Robert Taft, Jr. came up once and we've had film stars, Charlie Chaplin, Steward Granger, Ilka Chase—she wrote in a book about us. We had those beer people, the Busches I think they are, the ones with the game park or whatever in Florida. They came up with patches on their jackets advertising their monkey house or whatever.

"In sixty-four Kenyatta and Selassie came up. Selassie brought his famous chihuahua, the one he takes everywhere. He had no meat for the dog and finally opened a huge five-pound tin of beef and fed it to the bitty thing that must have weighed three pounds," said the tall man.

A bell rang at five o'clock.

"Tea and toast served on the roof. Tea for guests and toast for the baboons," said the tall man.

The elderly gentleman and the young woman drank tea on the roof of the hotel. Some other tourists drank tea on the roof of the hotel. The tourists watched water buffalo drink at the watering hole. Water buffalo drank at the watering hole. Baboons on the roof ate toast. The tourists watched the baboons.

"Oh my. Look what that monkey did," said a woman.

"Darn. That was my last Havana," said a man.

"We're over here on Adventures Unlimited. We booked the tour on the sixth floor of Abercrombie and Fitch," said a man,

"Our wives said they didn't want to come. They're home playing bridge. We'll show them films of the trip when we get back," said a man.

The young woman and the elderly gentleman ate a turkey dinner. The tourists were served a turkey dinner.

Rhinoceros, waterbuck, water buffalo and elephants drank at the watering hole. Rhinoceros, waterbuck, water buffalo and elephants ate leaves and grass at the watering hole. Tourists left the dining table to look at the rhinoceros, waterbuck, water buffalo and elephants eat leaves and grass. Floodlights were turned on. The floodlights illuminated the rhinoceros, waterbuck, water buffalo and elephants. The rhinoceros, waterbuck, water buffalo and elephants ate and drank. The elderly gentleman watched the rhinoceros, waterbuck, water buffalo and elephants from the window of his room. The elderly gentleman took photographs of the rhinoceros, waterbuck, water buffalo and elephants.

"Maybe I'll take closer shots at ground level. Yes, I think I'll go down on the ground. I'll go down where it's dark and try to sneak up close to them," said the elderly gentleman.

"Oh, I know you're supposed to stay in the hotel. You're not supposed to go down on the ground. Do you think you should?" said the young woman.

"No, I've decided. I'm going down anyway," said the elderly gentleman.

"You're so forceful," said the young woman.

"I hope I can get a good close-up of the way the elephants drink with their trunks. That's something to see," said the elderly gentleman.

"Don't you have a little fear?" said the young woman.

"I want to show you don't have to be afraid of wild animals," said the elderly gentleman.

"I think you're wonderful but you mustn't hurt yourself," said the young woman,

"Oh, I'll be careful," said the elderly gentleman.

The young woman kissed the elderly gentleman. The young woman caressed the face of the elderly gentleman. The young woman lay on the bed. The young woman smiled at the elderly gentleman.

"I'll be waiting. I think it's so exciting, to make love in the trees," said the young woman.

"All right," said the elderly gentleman.

The elderly gentleman climbed down the ladder.

The elderly gentleman approached the wild animals. The wild animals drank at the watering hole. The elderly gentleman took photographs of the wild animals drinking at the watering hole. An elephant roared. A rhinoceros grunted. A large rhinoceros pushed a small rhinoceros. The small rhinoceros pushed the large rhinoceros.

A waterbuck walked near the elderly gentleman. The waterbuck looked at the elderly gentleman. The elderly gentleman took photographs of the waterbuck. The waterbuck loped towards the elderly gentleman. The elderly gentleman walked rapidly away from the waterbuck. The waterbuck loped very near the elderly gentleman. The elderly gentleman stood behind a tree. The waterbuck stood very near the tree. The elderly gentleman looked at the waterbuck. The waterbuck looked at the elderly gentleman. The waterbuck walked away from the elderly gentleman.

The elderly gentleman climbed the ladder.

"I think I got some pretty good pictures. I was almost charged by a waterbuck," said the elderly gentleman.

"How awful," said the young woman.

"It was about five feet away," said the elderly gentleman.

"I could never go that near the animals," said the young woman.

"It wasn't much," said the elderly gentleman.

"Now we can make love. I'm glad you've finished with that business," said the young woman.

The elderly gentleman attempted to remove a cartridge of film from his camera. The elderly gentleman broke the cartridge of film.

"I'm going to have to go down there and take those pictures again. I just ruined the film," said the elderly gentleman.

"Oh, you're not going near those animals again, are you?" said the young woman.

"The animals don't bother me so much now that I've been close to them once," said the elderly gentleman.

"Maybe now you'll be too daring for your own good," said the young woman.

"It was pretty exciting. I'm glad I did it," said the elderly gentleman.

"It was just lucky you weren't injured. I'm afraid you won't be so lucky and might be injured if you go down there again," said the young woman.

"I want to go down again," said the elderly gentleman.

"Do you have to?" said the young woman.

"I'm going down," said the elderly gentleman.

"I have to admire you," said the young woman.

"I'd like to get a closer view of a rhinoceros this time. I think the pictures of the rhinoceros I took down there would've come out blurry," said the elderly gentleman.

The young woman embraced the elderly gentleman.

"I'm worried," said the young woman.

"I'll be careful," said the elderly gentleman.

"Dear," said the young woman.

The young woman kissed the elderly gentleman. The young woman caressed the elderly gentleman. The young woman lay on the bed. The young woman smiled at the elderly gentleman.

"I can't wait to make love in the trees," said the young woman.

"Well, I'll be back in a few minutes," said the elderly gentleman. The elderly gentleman climbed down the ladder.

The elderly gentleman approached the wild animals drinking at the watering hole. The elderly gentleman took photographs of the wild animals drinking at the watering hole. A rhinoceros grunted. A water buffalo shook its head. Another water buffalo shook its head. An elephant looked at the elderly gentleman. The elephant roared at the elderly gentleman. The elephant walked towards the elderly gentleman. The elderly gentleman walked away from the elephant. The elephant galloped towards the elderly gentleman. The elderly gentleman ran away from the elephant. The elephant galloped very near the elderly gentleman. The elephant galloped into the woods away from the elderly gentleman. Another elephant walked towards the elderly gentleman. The elderly gentleman walked away from the elephant. The elephant walked near the elderly gentleman, The elderly gentleman walked onto the bank of the watering hole away from the elephant. The elephant walked near the elderly gentleman. The elderly gentleman walked into the watering hole away from the elephant. The elderly gentleman sank to his knees in the mud in the watering hole. The elderly gentleman stuck fast in the mud of the watering hole. The elephant stood near the elderly gentleman in the watering hole. The tall man climbed down the ladder. The tall man walked to the watering hole. The tall man pulled the elderly man from the watering hole. The tall man and the elderly man climbed the ladder.

"I'll get you some shoes and trousers in the morning. Those won't be dry," said the tall man.

"I'm so glad he isn't injured. I told him he was foolish going so near the animals," said the young woman.

"I was positive that elephant was going to finish me off in the water. I couldn't move. The one that charged me almost did finish me off," said the elderly gentleman.

"How horrible," said the young woman.

"Thanks for the hand," said the elderly gentleman.

"Not a bit. Any time," said the tall man.

"You should be more careful. You're such an adventurous man," said the young woman.

"I admit I was pretty scared. But I didn't let it get the better of me," said the elderly gentleman.

"You're such a level-headed man," said the young woman.

The young woman kissed the neck of the elderly gentleman. The young woman kissed the eyes of the elderly gentleman. The young woman smiled at the elderly gentleman. The young woman lay on the bed.

"Now we can make love," said the young woman.

"Yes, we might as well do that," said the elderly gentleman.

"I've never made love in a treehouse before," said the young woman.

"No, I guess I haven't either," said the elderly gentleman.

The elderly gentleman lay in the bed. The young woman made love to the elderly gentleman. The elderly gentleman made love to the young woman. The young woman made love to the elderly gentleman. The elderly gentleman made love to the young woman. The elderly gentleman and the young woman fell asleep. The young woman woke up. The young women woke up the elderly gentleman. The young woman made love to the elderly gentleman. The elderly gentleman made love to the young woman. The elderly gentleman and the young woman fell asleep. The young woman woke up. The young woman woke up the elderly gentleman. The young woman made love to the elderly gentleman. The elderly gentleman made love to the young woman. The elderly gentleman told the young woman he wished she would not wake him up again during the night. The elderly gentleman said he did not want to make love again during the night. The elderly gentleman said he did not feel like making love again during the night. The elderly gentleman said that after making love as much as he had during the night he did not feel well enough to make love again during the night. The elderly gentleman and the young woman fell asleep.

A bell rang at seven o'clock in the morning.

"I'll have the boys put together a box that'll be quite adequate to carry him at least to Nairobi," said the tall man.

"Yes," said the young woman.

"Doubtless he himself never woke up if you say he didn't wake you. It's really the best way you know. Never knew what was happening to him.

"A heart attack almost certainly, it looks to me. I suppose the fright of that business of the elephants was just a bit more than he could stand at his age," said the tall man.

"Yes," said the young woman.

"Say, but I am very sorry about all this," said the tall man.

"Yes. Yes, I'm very sorry about it too," said the young woman.

THREE

DIGNITY

The King lived in a hotel. The suite of the King was on the third floor of the hotel. The hotel overlooked the Saronic Gulf. The hotel was sixteen miles south of Athens. The furnishings of the bedroom of the suite were ordinary except for an oversized bed. The King was over six feet tall and required an oversized bed. The other three rooms of the suite were three living rooms decorated in matching shades of red. The furnishings of the three living rooms were ordinary. The other one hundred forty-six rooms of the hotel were occupied by the King's retinue.

The King was Saud bin Abdulaziz. The King had been King of Saudi Arabia for eleven years. The King had been deposed by his brother King Faisal in 1964. The King had once ruled more than eight million people. Now the King led a secluded life. At dawn each day the King dressed in flowing robes and faced east towards the sea and gave thanks to Allah. Then the King was massaged. After breakfast the King met with his private secretary and son-in-law, Abdul Rahman Abdulaziz el-Ghuneim. The King spent the remainder of the morning with women of his entourage. Before lunch the King drove to Piraeus to swim in the indoor pool. In the evening the King received visitors. After dinner the King sat in the hotel garden with his sons and men of his retinue and listened to them tell stories and sing Bedouin songs. The King had once owned the most famous stables in the East and especially enjoyed listening to stories about horses and equestrian feats. One day thirty of the King's sons and daughters whom he had not seen in two years came to the hotel. The King said he expected his court to increase to three hundred people. The King planned to make long cruises to the Greek Islands. The King went on outings. The King's favorite outings were picnics in grassy meadows full of wildflowers near the sea. The King played with his youngest daughter, six-year-old Princess Nouzha, when he had free time.

The King said little about his business interests or the politics of his country. A member of the retinue listened to news broadcasts on the radio and informed the King of major world events.

"I love my country but my dignity is above all else," said the King.

The Greek government provided an official escort for the King. A police car accompanied the King wherever he went.

"It is this car which pleases me above everything else in my life in Greece," said the King. "This car is an official honor of the government. I am very happy. Sometimes I am allowed even to ride inside of this car."

THE KING AND HIS COURT

The King sat with his court. The King sat drinking with members of his court in the bar of the Hotel Eden. The King and three members of his court drank cocktails at a table of the rooftop bar of the Hotel Eden and looked at the view from the roof of the Hotel Eden. It was a very pretty view.

It was a very pretty view of the Villa Borghese and the Pincio Gardens. In the city there was very pleasant weather. A short waiter told the King that he believed that the next day there would also be very pleasant weather. The King nodded. The King agreed that the next day there would probably also be very pleasant weather.

The short waiter patted the King. He patted the King's arm and told the King it was a tragedy and it was certain that the King would soon be restored to the throne of his country. The King shrugged. The King did not know whether he would soon be restored to the throne of his country.

At the table of the bar the courtier Papagos drank cocktails and talked into the King's ear. The King did not listen to what the courtier Papagos said. Another courtier drank cocktails and stroked his long moustache with long fingers and picked at his long nose.

The King was a tall and very handsome young man. In the bar of the Hotel Eden the King wore dark glasses and alligator shoes. With his court in the bar of the Hotel Eden looking at the very pretty view in the very pleasant weather the King drank from a cocktail and pouted sadly.

A man approached the table of the King and his court in the bar of the Hotel Eden.

"Are you the King?" the man asked the King.

"He is not the King," the courtier Papagos said to the man.

"He looks like the King," said the man.

"He is not the King," said the courtier Papagos. "The King has nothing to say. He is another person. The King is at another place."

The King asked the man who he was. The man told the King who he was.

"I suppose I am the King," said the King.

The King stood up. The King's courtiers stood up. The King said hello to the man and shook hands with the man.

The King said he was happy to meet the man. The King had read a book written by the man. The King had thought when he read the book he would be happy to meet the man who had written the book. Now the King had met the man.

The man said he was happy to meet the King. Now he had met the King.

The King invited the man to sit at the table among the members of his court.

The King sat down. The King's courtiers sat down.

"The King will say nothing. The King has nothing to say. The King will not discuss politics," said the courtier Papagos.

The man asked the King what was his opinion of the draft constitution of the ruling junta.

"The King has no opinion of the so-called constitution," said the courtier Papagos.

"I do not know what to think about this," said the King, "It is difficult for me to know what to think about these things. I suppose it would be better for our country if there was democracy. As for what it says about the King, I suppose it is not very bad."

"It is very bad," said the courtier Papagos.

The King drank some of his vodka cocktail.

"I suppose I would like for them to put in another ice," said the King. "I could ask them for another ice."

"The King drinks rarely," said the courtier Papagos. "The King comes to this place rarely. The suite of this hotel is merely in order for the King to deal with his mail. The King comes to this place merely once a week to deal with mail. The King has very large quarters elsewhere.

"The King has no opinion. The King's opinions are not to be reported. You must swear to absolute secrecy. The King regards very seriously the appearance of inaccurate publicity.

"You must appreciate that matters are now extremely delicate. It is possible that representatives of the King negotiate with the so-called government. Perhaps there are discussions about provisions of the so-called constitution which pertain to the return of the King.

"Of course, to speak in confidence, it is necessary to say that there is no limit to the King's scorn for the illegal government of the April putsch. It is a brutal and fascist government which the King would easily have overthrown in December except for the heinous treachery of a few.

"It is criminally traitorous to propose a constitution which destroys the power of the King to appoint members of the government. It is also impossible for the King not to be commander of the army. Of course it is outrageous and unacceptable that the government should have responsibility for educating the Crown Prince.

"There can be no compromise with such proposals. The King is confident the government will come to its senses."

The man asked the King if he intended returning to his country to reign under the terms of the constitution.

"The King will not make another statement," said the courtier Papagos. "The King has made his statement of December. The King has demanded the re-establishment of normal democratic political life in his country before he will consent to undertake the burdens of again leading his people."

"I do not know about this," said the King. "Perhaps it would be better without a king."

"The King is strained," said the courtier Papagos. "There has been a great trial for the King. It is unthinkable for there not to be King, It is unthinkable for anyone to be king but the King."

The man asked the King what he did while he was in Italy.

"I do not do anything," said the King,

"The King is very busy," said the courtier Papagos. "The King constantly prepares for his return to his homeland. The King works always with great energy to save his country."

The man asked the King how he liked living in Italy.

"I would be very happy to live in Italy another time," said the King. "Now I am very sad to live here. I am very sad for my wife. My wife was very sad. You are aware in December my wife lost the child. The doctors say it was something else but no, I say it was sadness. She had become very sad because of the adventure of December.

"The adventure of December makes me very sad. I was certain that it would be impossible for me to replace the government. Mama said it would not be difficult for me to replace the government. Mama and the others believed it was necessary for me to replace the government."

"The King will not discuss these matters," said the courtier Papagos. "Other matters will now be discussed."

The courtier Papagos asked the man who was to be elected President of the United States. The courtier Papagos was very interested to know who was to be the next President of the United States. The King did not know that Nelson Rockefeller was a candidate to be President of the United States.

"I do not know much about these things," said the King. "Really I do not like politics."

The man asked the King what he intended doing now.

"I do not know what I will do," said the King. "I suppose I will wait and see what will happen."

"The King will very soon be king," said the courtier Papagos. "If there is agreement with the government perhaps it will be possible for the King to reconsider his attitude with regard to the misguided persons who have foolishly and recklessly imposed dictatorship upon our poor country."

The man talked with the King. The King liked Italian food. The King and the Queen ate at many restaurants in the city. The King and the Queen liked to attend motion pictures in the city. The King and the Queen attended motion pictures in the city very often. The King and the Queen watched television.

The King invited the man to meet with him at the Olgiata Club fifteen miles north of the city. The King was very sad. The King would be happier if the man met with him at the Olgiata Club.

"The King will be unable to meet with you," said the courtier Papagos.

"There is no time in which the King is able to meet with persons. The King is always too busy to meet with persons. The King is very happy."

The King said there was a very sublime motion picture playing in the city that evening. The King said he would like very much to see that evening the sublime motion picture with the Queen. The King said he would like very much to see "Gone with the Wind" with the Queen that evening.

The King sat with two women. The King sat drinking with two old women at a table on the terrace of the clubhouse of the Olgiata Club. At the table under an umbrella on the terrace of the clubhouse of the Olgiata Club the King and the two old women drank cocktails and looked at a kite. A boy flew a kite above the golf course of the Olgiata Club. The kite was red.

One of the old women did not know how it was possible for kites to fly. The King was unable to explain to the old woman how it was possible for kites to fly. The King did not understand how it was possible for a kite to fly. Yet above the golf course of the Olgiata Club the red kite flew.

The old women were Americans and drank cocktails and told the King how happy they were to have met the King. They were very happy to meet kings and had met many kings. Wearing wide straw hats and jangling bracelets the old women sat on the terrace of the clubhouse of the Olgiata Club with the King and played dominoes with each other.

One of the old women asked the King if he would like another cocktail. The King was uncertain whether he would like another cocktail. The old woman brought another cocktail from the bar of the clubhouse of the Olgiata Club to the King. In front of the King on the table under the umbrella there were many empty cocktail glasses.

Sitting at a table under an umbrella on the terrace of the clubhouse of the Olgiata Club looking at a red kite with the two old women the King wept silently.

"I wish I could do something to help," said one of the old women. "It's so sad."

One of the old women handed the King her handkerchief.

The man approached the table of the King and the old women on the terrace of the clubhouse of the Olgiata Club.

The King stood up. The old women stood up. The King shook hands with the man. Although the King was weeping he was happy to meet the man again. It was necessary for the King to meet so many men he was not happy to meet. There was a bandage on the King's lip.

"This is the King," said one of the old women.

"His car hit a tree," said the other old woman.

The King invited the man to sit down at the table among the old women.

The King sat down. The old women sat down.

The King drank some of his cocktail. The King wept and wiped tears from his eyes.

"The King's not a happy man," said one of the old women.

"The King's been drinking," said the other old woman.

"You must forgive me," said the King. "I am very sad. I know I should not be crying. You will pay no attention to me. You cannot imagine. It is on account of Mama. I do not like to talk like this but I tell the truth.

"I tell you Mama is a devil. You do not know the trouble of becoming king again. I would be king still. Mama says I must be king again. You will excuse me. You will not think of me. We are an emotional people. You do not know what it is to be responsible for the death of a little one."

"I don't know if you should talk about your mother that way," said one of the old women.

"You just go right ahead and cry, Your Highness," said the other old woman. "It's good for you to relieve yourself."

The King wiped tears from his eyes and smiled. "You are sweet ladies," said the King.

The King blew his nose. One of the old women told the King a joke about a duke. The King laughed. The King believed the joke to be funny.

The King was uncertain whether he would like another cocktail. One of the old women brought another cocktail from the bar of the clubhouse of the Olgiata Club to the King.

"We've come to know His Highness so well," said one of the old women. "We really feel we're a part of the royal court."

The man asked the King if he ever played golf on the golf course of the Olgiata Club.

"I do not like to play golf," said the King. "I play golf a little. Mama says it is good if I play golf. I took lessons in golf. The teachers say I am very good at golf."

The man said he understood the King's quarters were somewhere on the grounds of the Olgiata Club,

The King pointed at a small villa of red plaster nearby.

"The rent is very high," said the King. "But the house is very nice. There is very good heating. The Queen and the children enjoy the house very much. The Queen and the children enjoy the courtyard although it is a small courtyard."

The King pointed at a large villa of white marble on a hill in the distance overlooking the grounds of the Olgiata Club.

"That is the house of Mama and the Princess," said the King. "It has been loaned to them by a very rich man from our country. It is a very beautiful house. There is a very large courtyard."

The man asked the King if he had traveled very much since it had been necessary for him to leave his country.

"I prefer not to travel," said the King. "Mama prefers to travel. We traveled twice to Copenhagen to visit the family of the Queen. Each weekend we travel to Ischia by yacht. I traveled to Rimini. Mama said it was necessary for me to travel to Rimini. Mama said it was necessary for me to lay a wreath to honor the graves of soldiers of our country in Rimini."

"I think it was lovely to do that," said one of the old women.

"I traveled to London," said the King, "It was necessary for me to take the Prince to the eye doctor. I traveled to the doctor in Switzerland. England and Switzerland are very beautiful countries. I suffer very much from sinusitis."

"It's not fair," said one of the old women. "His Highness has had to suffer from so much."

"I do not prefer to go to parties," said the King. "I would prefer to go to a small number of big parties instead of to many small parties. I go to many small parties with my relatives. I have many relatives in Italy. I go to small parties with my aunts in Florence. My aunts in Florence refuse to go to big parties."

"The King's talking about the Queen Mother of Rumania and the Duchess of Aosta, you know," said one of the old women. "I think it's mean of them to do that."

A limousine approached the clubhouse of the Olgiata Club from the direction of the villa of white marble. The King pointed at the limousine.

"My soul," said the King. "It is Mama."

The Queen Mother approached the table of the King and the man and the old women on the terrace of the clubhouse of the Olgiata Club. In her hat the Queen Mother wore flowers. The flowers were of either of two colors. The colors were the national colors of her country.

The King stood up. The man stood up. The old women stood up. A servant followed the Queen Mother at a distance. The servant carried a bowl of fruit.

The King invited the Queen Mother to sit at the table with the man and the old women. The King sat down. The old women sat down. The Queen Mother did not sit down.

"Stand up," said the Queen Mother. "Why are you here? Now you should be making preparations. You do nothing properly. Where is Papagos? I see you have drunk too much."

The King stood up. The old women stood up.

"I do not think I have drunk too much," said the King. "I have drunk a little."

"Too much," said the Queen Mother.

"The King just drank one or two cocktails," said one of the old women.

"Too much," said the Queen Mother.

The Queen Mother sat down. The King sat down. The man sat down. The old women sat down. The servant sat down behind the Queen Mother.

"You will leave at once," said the Queen Mother. "You will make preparations at once."

"Yes, Mama," said the King. "I will leave."

The King told the man and the old women that he was to meet with a man from his country. The man was an important politician of his country who worked secretly to make it possible for the King to return to his country under favorable conditions. Now the man was to fly to Italy to secretly meet with the King. The King and the courtier Papagos were to secretly meet in disguise with the man at a secret location.

"I love mysteries," said one of the old women.

"At once," said the Queen Mother.

The Queen Mother stood up. The man and the old women and the servant stood up. The King did not stand up.

"You will stand up," said the Queen Mother. "You will leave at once."

The King drank some of his cocktail.

"I am very tired," said the King, "I am leaving."

"At once," said the Queen Mother.

The Queen Mother plucked at the King's sleeve. The King's cocktail spilled on the table.

"You are leaving at once," said the Queen Mother. "You will stand up at once and leave or I will tell George to carry you."

The King stood up.

"I am leaving," said the King. The King pouted sadly.

"You will drink coffee," said the Queen Mother.

"I do not think you should pull my arm," said the King.

"He's the King," said one of the old women.

"If you do not leave at once I will pull your nose," said the Queen Mother. "Give me something," said the Queen Mother to the servant.

The servant took an apple from the bowl of fruit and offered it to the Queen Mother.

"Not that," said the Queen Mother.

The servant took a pear from the bowl of fruit and offered it to the Queen Mother, The Queen Mother took the pear. The Queen Mother began to eat the pear. It was a juicy pear.

The courtier Papagos walked from the clubhouse of the Olgiata Club. The courtier Papagos approached the table of the King and the man and the old women on the terrace of the clubhouse of the Olgiata Club. He wore a false moustache

"The King and I will leave at once," said the courtier Papagos. "I have the King's disguise. The car is ready."

"This is so exciting," said one of the old women.

A page summoned the courtier Papagos to the clubhouse of the Olgiata Club. There was an urgent telephone call for the courtier Papagos. The courtier Papagos soon returned to the table of the King and the man and the old women.

"It is not necessary for the King to leave," said the courtier Papagos. "There has been an unfortunate event. The man has been arrested. The police of the so-called government ruthlessly dragged him from the airplane before it took off. The usurpers have imprisoned him at the police station."

"Oh my," said one of the old women. "That's a shame."

The courtier Papagos removed the false moustache and put it in his pocket.

The Queen sat down. The King sat down. The man and the old women and the servant and the courtier Papagos sat down.

The King and the Queen Mother and the man and the old women and the courtier Papagos talked. One of the old women brought another cocktail from the bar of the clubhouse of the Olgiata Club to the King. The Queen Mother was angry with the government of her country and complained about it.

"The Queen Mother's opinions are not to be reported," said the courtier Papagos, "The King has nothing to say."

The Queen Mother stood up. The King and the man and the old women and the servant and the courtier Papagos stood up.

The Queen Mother talked with the courtier Papagos about the government and the constitution and the monarchy. The Queen Mother walked with the courtier Papagos into a tulip garden. The servant walked into the tulip garden. Following the Queen Mother at a distance the servant carried the bowl of fruit into the tulip garden.

The King sat down. The man sat down. The old women sat down.

At the table under the umbrella on the terrace of the clubhouse of the Olgiata Club the King and the man and the old women drank cocktails and talked about the weather and the King wept a little.

"Would you like to have a medal?" the King asked the man. "I have many medals if you would like to have a medal."

The King would have preferred to live in Portugal or Switzerland. In Portugal or Switzerland there were many former kings and queens. In Portugal or Switzerland the King would have preferred to open a restaurant.

FOUR

POLITICS

The four Americans in Beirut were discussing the political events of Iraq and Syria.

A Kurd had told one of the Americans that relations between the new government of Ahmed Hassan al-Bakr in Iraq and the Kurdish nationalists of General Mustafa al-Barzani had become much worse. The Kurd had told the American that General Amin el-Hafez and Mansour el-Atrash had installed themselves in Mosul in northern Iraq. The Kurd had said that there were rumors in Baghdad that General Hafez and Mansour el-Atrash would attempt to overthrow the leftist Baath government of Syria. The Kurds believed that the government in Baghdad would avoid a contest with General el-Barzani until after the Syrian question was settled. General Hafez and Mr. al-Bakr were close friends. They were moderate Baathists who strongly opposed the leftist Baathists who had driven General Hafez from power in a coup d'etat in Damascus in February 1966. Mansour el-Atrash was the son of Sultan el-Atrash, feudal chief of Druse Mountain in southern Syria. Oddly, the army officer who had mounted the attack on General Hafez's residence was a Druse, Lieutenant Colonel Selim Hatoum. But late in 1966 Colonel Hatoum had turned against the new government and had attempted to overthrow it but had failed and fled to Jordan. During the Arab-Israeli war of June 1967 Colonel Hatoum had returned to Syria and put himself under the protection of Sultan el-Atrash, who was his feudal chief and had offered his services to the Syrian Army. The Syrian *government had summoned Colonel Hatoum to Damascus and had arrested him, summarily tried him and executed him. The Druse officers of the Syrian Army had walked away from the front in protest. The Kurds had told the American that the Kurds were not concerned with the contest between the moderate and extremist Baathists except as it could affect the Baghdad government's policy towards the Kurds. He had said that on the night of July 20 after the second coup d'etat when Mr. al-Bakr had been made Premier as well as President, Mr. al-Bakr had met for several hours with Mohsen Desaee and Habib Murad, who is known as "Barzani's secretary." Mr. al-Bakr had agreed that there would be four Kurdish cabinet ministers, three of them to be chosen by General al-Barzani and one chosen by the government but not from among adherents of Jalal Talabani, who was regarded by Barzanist Kurds as a government agent. Mr. al-Bakr had agreed the government would proclaim the next day that it would negotiate a settlement of the Kurdish question with general al-Barzani on the basis of the twelve points enunciated in June 1966 by Abdel Rahman al-Bazzaz, which provided for local autonomy for the Kurds. Mohsen Desaee and Ihsan Shirzade had been appointed cabinet ministers on July 31.*

But Mr. al-Bakr had made no announcement of negotiations and on August 4 had appointed Tahar Mohieddin, a Talabanist Kurd, Minister of State, so that Mohsen Desaee and Ihsan Shirzade had refused to take the oath of office.

"This is what I find difficult to understand," said one of the Americans.

"Al-Bakr is a puzzle," said another American.

"I don't understand any of it," said another American.

The other American shrugged his shoulders.

"Politicians are selfish men," he said.

THE RENEGADE

Idealism in anything is a vice, but in politics it is a misfortune.

—wise old man

There is something with a traditional form in Russia. It is connected absolutely with Russian czarism. This is the continuation of czarist bureaucracy. The Czech crisis could not have been avoided. There was nothing that American policy might have done. In such conditions there was nothing. But if there were no Viet Nam, if France were active, if the Czechs had fought. The fact is we see now that any revolution cannot change a nation and the tendencies and the dualities and traits of a nation but changes only the form of power and property but not the nation itself.

When they send me to jail in 1956 for the first time they try to break me. This is psychological and not physical. This is the worst time of my life. I would rather go insane than to break. I can tell you about Stalin if you were his friend he was very nice, very agreeable to you, very frank. This man had a very good personality and was engaging with great humor. However towards others he is completely ruthless. This is very bad. I had the possibility to see Stalin several times in Moscow. Physically I had no criticism because these prisons are very sanitary and progressive with medical care.

Marxism, Leninism today in the world do not exist. This is true. You cannot find a Marxist country. There is in certain places a smaller difference between the rich and poor, this is true. Marxism predicts the creation of the new man.

I believe America will go near socialism. Perhaps some oppose this who speak much about the doctrine of free enterprise. However I believe that most of these will understand that it is impossible to achieve democracy which they support without socialism. I say this because in America I see there is great concern for the individual. The new man is exactly the old man. It is a mistake. A new man cannot be produced only by the change of social organization.

I thought in myself, why is such a country of far social advancement such as America not a socialist country. I think about my theories and modified them. You see, America does not prove the ideas of Marx. There is some going back to Stalinism but I think this formulation of neo-Stalinism is too strong. They take some steps backward but at the same time they take opposite steps from Stalinism. For example, in the economy they made some reforms which are contrary to Stalinist methods. At the same time they did not break with legality. I think this is a situation of moral stagnation rather than neo-Stalinism.

There is the repressive power of the state. Not only. I think this ruling group in Soviet Russia, the ruling stratum, this Soviet party bureaucracy, is more consolidated and at the same time represents conservative force, a conservative tendency of a very great nation, and this is the problem in Russia. I am a communist, yes, certainly. From the earliest time against the King I was a communist in my country.

Always I was against the existence of exploitation of workers. This principle is always in the center of my life.

However we have ideology which says that it is communist but this does not resemble the historical ideology or theory. This communism must be changed to a better communism, which perhaps will not be called communism. Without resolving their problems, that means problems of democracy, problems of Russian bureaucracy, that means the opening of possibilities to the Russian nation of new perspectives in the world, a new role in the world, there can be no easy change in Russia.

True Marxism as it has been described by Marx, is it possible for this to exist anywhere in the world? Communism is created but many things remain. What has been changed? Merely that some men have been killed and men have power taken from them and given to others. The power itself does not change and this should happen.

The bureaucratic class will not be eliminated by violence but slowly by education and conversations. It will be possible to persuade the bureaucrats to perform other work which is more valuable. I think the Soviet Union is in the same process as any other Eastern European country. The difference only is in level and in the deepness, but not in quality. I see in Russia also this changing must go more slowly and not so easily as in other Eastern European countries. I must tell you these bureaucrats are dull men whose work is dull and it will be possible to give them interesting work which they will enjoy to do and which they will be persuaded follows a better ideology.

I wish to make precise one question. The decadence of Marxist-Leninist ideology does not mean the decadence of all those societies in Eastern Europe. Those societies are in some internal conflicts but not in decadence. Production is going up with some difficulties typical for those countries, but technology is developing. Culture is developing on a very large scale. The people triumph over their rulers. These people, the New Leftists, if you ask them what is their purpose and they answer you they do not know, only to destroy what exists. But progress in Eastern Europe is impossible without changing the old-fashioned political and social atmosphere.

That is, there is the complete absence of ideology and they will even tell you this. Always when I was young and at every moment since then I have the idea before me of what should be done. This is everything to me, the ideology which I work for. Therefore, as to this group as we find it in France and elsewhere, these people have absolutely no perspective of success.

The motivation of Russian policy is socialism. This is not Russian chauvinism and a desire to expand in the area. But Leninism of today becomes Russian nationalism, because there is nothing creative in this Leninism nor any new ideas. The czars say they spread Orthodoxy but they did not believe this but the form was favorable for deceiving the people. But this was the despotism and madness such as Hitler's. In the invasion of Czechoslovakia you see unquestionably before your eyes the absolute bankruptcy of the accepted ideology. This forgetting the right of self-determination of an entire nation, I see this a criminal act in the highest degree.

I break with Tito, I think, soon after the death of Stalin. I was dissatisfied with policy. We began to have disagreements over ideology when I wrote certain criticisms of government administration. Yet all the time I want only to be positive to help the country.

The possibility that the Russians will intervene in Yugoslavia as in Czechoslovakia I do not think exists. I do not believe in immediate danger for Yugoslavia from this Soviet policy that it has the right to intervene in any socialist country. My complaints never mention Tito but this is a man who does not appreciate criticism of any kind. He is I will say a little bit unreasonable person. If a Russian attack comes, we will fight. After Tito even without the possibility of the solidarity of the old partisans we would fight as a nation. There in no prospect for a pro-Russian government.

Today I am very happy. You are happy when you work for a good thing which will be positive for the people and which will encourage their rights which they have not been allowed to use. To work for freedom, to work for the society which uses the correct ideology, to construct the correct ideology. Injustice is the result from ignorance and bad habits of tradition which has not been challenged. It is very good for me to be able to perceive the faults of the political systems of today.

Perhaps if the Czechs had mobilized, if they had fought, perhaps the Russians would not have attacked. But this is something which we cannot decide. The Czechs have feelings which we cannot know. Yet I think it would have been better.

I did not want to take any power. I saw no reason to want to head the government then. Yet Tito in his accusation said this. What is important is ideas, policies, not the control of administration. This does not interest me so much.

The present Russian leadership is not haunted by fear of encirclement as the Soviet Union under Stalin. They do not even fear Germany. What we find today is the possibility of destruction of the world through misunderstanding. This is battle with hydrogen bombs between countries which attack each other's ideology. They fear Germany only as a nation which may be united with some other under fascist ideology. But in fact the ideologies are not so different if you compare the practices instead of beliefs. This would be the greatest tragedy if the world would end through this mistake of ideologies. Except for this ideology difference there would be no chance of this happening. It is so clear that Germany does not think of threatening. The Russians are not stupid. They do not fear this.

From where does the power of the United States arrive? It is not from her wealth—perhaps this is something—but it is her ideas, her ideas of democracy and freedom. What is the power of the Soviet Union? This is the power of the good ideas of communism.

When he was in power, I was sometimes critical of Khrushchev but I think Khrushchev was better than this government. He was a more bold man, maybe with strong contradictions in his person. He was really a reformer. He made some serious achievement for the Soviet Union. I think in Vietnam that definitely the United States made a mistake in this.

The North Vietnamese try to control the south, this is true. But still this should have been resisted by the people if this is their wish. The communists wish to impose their will on some people who do not wish to have a socialist arrangement. I despise terrorism and there have been crimes. Mao attempts evidently to destroy bureaucracy, the apparatus of the Party, but which is the worse, the bureaucracy of vicious anarchy, private feud, evident in Sinkiang? This lack of planning cannot but harm the people and social progress. There is never excuse for murder, coercion, torture. There is only one rule in relations between people and this is toleration.

I believe the presence of the Americans has become an imposition although the Americans did not plan this to happen. There are peasant habits in Viet Nam which are anti-democratic. These can be altered through education. In China ideology becomes merely the façade of personal dispute and this is the greatest corruption because all factions say they are loyal to Mao. It is impossible to participate in orderly government. True, the bureaucracy is to be feared and destroyed. Also, I believe because the United States is strong in armies it uses these things of force too much. America should persuade. There should be moral appeal. America's intentions are good I believe.

I do not foresee the possibility of a loyal opposition within the Soviet Communist Party. Not for the near future. I am speaking of a Marxist Russia as such. The fact of a war in Viet Nam created an international atmosphere in which the Soviet action against Czechoslovakia was possible. It was favorable for Russia. As the war continued, the Russians started to play on the contradictions between China and the United States. This is my opinion. It is true force sometimes must be used. This is to prevent use of force against you because force is used in ignorance as with Russia or madness such as Hitler. However I think it is possible to propagate an ideology of peace throughout all nations which is the same as the commandment of not killing among individuals which will make it impossible to think of war. China is a different question from Yugoslavia because China is a great ideological power. The Russians are not stupid. They know very well that this split in Communism between China and them is definite. It is deeper than the split with Yugoslavia. If the war in Viet Nam had not been raging that would have been much more favorable for the Czechs if you mean the reformist movement in Eastern Europe. I think reformist movements are of the greatest historical importance because no one can stop them and these movements are opening a new perspective of relations between Western countries and the Eastern. That means, collaboration, similarity of ideas.

And they cannot find, I am convinced, compromise on an ideological basis. That means they never will be people with the same ideas. It is not a question of sharing historical, even some national rights, for example to Mongolia and some parts of Siberia. On Brioni we sat at a table and Tito asks me to defend to the others a policy for industry.

I understand this very little and there are some features that go against my ideas. I was the head of agit-prop. It is a session of the Central Committee. So I speak about Tito's ideas but also in such a way that I express also my ideas. Tito objects to this. From this time I begin to suspect that our ideas are going to differ.

To be in jail is really a good thing. Perhaps not for so long as ten years. It gives a man the time for thinking about his moral questions, his moral destiny, to decide for himself his goals, to clarify his ideas.

I think it will be easier for the United States to work and live with a nonrevolutionary nation than with a Soviet nation that was really revolutionary. But under some conditions— that means you must be strong in ideas and at the same time you must understand Russia. That means you must collaborate with Russia culturally and in economics and try to find the solution of existing problems such as nonproliferation, the German question and the Middle East question. When I was first in jail my mind worked harder than usual as compensation perhaps for the prison.

We must begin to cooperate. The world suffers very badly from the competition and factionalism, the contest of man against man. These energies instead must be used for useful and positive achievement. The instinct of competition is only habit and can be erased through education. The negative energies that are devoted now to the diminution of the other man must be used productively for the benefit of the whole of humanity.

The Church in the Eastern countries has come more to accept the ideas of socialism. They are more progressive in this than in the past. There are some points of Christian ideology which I do not favor but there are many solid ones. Of course I am an atheist. What is to be achieved I believe is the freedom of the person to do what he wishes as much as can be. He must have the choice of democracy and he must have no one to tell him what he must do. The person must come first. I believe the Christian ideology could be propagated better by something besides the Church. It is not necessary to have the complicated institution which the Church has created for this purpose and also all the clerical occupations.

Above all we must work for universal final abolition of wars. If you observe the products of war you find that they have led to nothing. Nothing has been achieved for the winner or loser which could not have been achieved more easily in another way. The big influence in Russia of the peasant class makes the struggle for change much different qualitatively than in Eastern Europe. There are great differences if you compare Yugoslavia with Soviet Europe. Yugoslavia is a European country. The Russians are part of Europe but a special part mixed with Asia. Asiatic despotism is a factor which is hurting the development of Russia. Even this can be overcome. Look at your history. Count the money you have spent to rehabilitate the territories which were destroyed. I think Russian nationalism is now deep even among communists. This ruling group is the element that is the most undemocratic in Russia. It is a hideous impulse of man to destroy another man. It is impossible I think for a man to be truly happy if there is not the possibility of equal happiness in another man.

I do not fear to go back now. Now I am not isolated, I have many friends. I was forbidden to publish for five years but two years of this is now used up. I have even a better apartment than before. My personal assessment of Tito, this is very contradictory. On one day I think one thing, on another day, another. But, generally, I regard him as a historic person. Especially in critical situations he is good. In the war, in the struggle against Stalinism, even now he is against the Czech occupation.

I think a nonmodel society will be the future society for Eastern Europe and the West. A nonmodel society means a society that we can not formulate as we can say, for example, what was capitalism in the nineteenth century or communism or socialism in the twentieth. We may very clearly describe this society, for example, as a private-property society, not a society of state or national or social property. Industrialization is good, yes. But there is danger. This is destruction of the personality of the factory worker in conformism and mechanization. A man must not become no more than a small wheel in a large machine which is to produce things.

Justice is the first thing. This must come first. It must be absolute or nothing else remains. This means fair play and also love of the right thing and to do what is right. He sent me to jail under charge of disloyalty to communism, of being a renegade, but this charge was not proved and the trial was not genuine. This oppression began to make me think again of this regime. I think that development is going on in both of these societies in the direction of nonmodel society—that does not mean that these societies will be in every way the same but not much difference. For example there now exists a mixed economy—that means private, public and cooperative forms.

My personal relations with Tito were excellent before our quarrel. We were close, like father and son. Maybe that was the reason our conflict was so sharp. I never really spoke against him personally at any time. Of course in my writing I criticized the system and he created most of it but I never personally was against him and I was never against his ruling the Party. My health is weak. I am alive and my health is sufficient to carry on my work. I do not ask for more than this. I believe I am very lucky to enjoy life for so many years even if some of this time has been in prison. It is true now I am able to make no money in Yugoslavia. I am able to live.

I see and believe that conflict between the growing educated class in the Soviet Union and the bureaucratic dictatorship is inevitable. I believe that this new New Class, this techno-structure class as Galbraith calls it, is the class of the future in Eastern Socialist countries and in Russia. I am optimistic in the victory of this class. I am convinced this class will win and we are at the beginning of the end of party bureaucracy in every communist country.

After Tito, I foresee a time of collective leadership. At the present stage of development of Yugoslavia, I do not believe the rule of only one man is necessary. Besides this, I could not understand that any man would want this job. I believe now everywhere in nations there will be evolution away from the ascendancy of a single man because there is too much to do.

I will continue to write. I believe soon I will be able to publish my opinion. I feel certain of this. I think the authorities will discover that what I say is the truth. You cannot compare Tito with Stalin because he is not so morbid and not such a cruel man. I think Tito, in our epoch, is in fourth place in communism. That is, Lenin, Stalin, Mao and Tito. Those are four great, great persons who created something new in communism. They will see that it is ridiculous to call my writing counterrevolutionary.

This social stratum, which I called New Class in my book, is absolutely in decadence, not only in the ideology but are also a parasitic social phenomenon. I believe classes can give up power without a savage fight. I can not only say, I am sure about not only Russia but in all other communist countries, this class will be changed without civil war. Perhaps there could be a personal reconciliation between me and Tito.

We are not far apart. I don't know what he is thinking. I feel that we are now not so against each other. I cannot say that we are friends, but I cannot say that we are enemies. Without civil war, maybe with some small insurrections and very large demonstrations such as we have experienced in Hungary, Czechoslovakia and Yugoslavia. They are different but the results are more or less similar.

I will say the question was this, what is the justification of power, of position? You have certain rulers everywhere, true. But they cannot just exist. They must exist for the good of the people. They must operate for the good of the people in a better way than any other or immediately their justification collapses.

But what was the situation? Here you have a group, a class, which operates more and more in justification of itself, of its possessions, villas, official cars, salaries, honors, and is thinking always of itself and not of the people. This to me is the only question of society. My son has become one of the very best students at the University. He becomes an electronic engineer and they let him work in an electric factory in Zagreb.

It is much better than if I held a high position now because my friends are much better. I believe my success will become greater all the time now. Certain points which I made before I am certain become more and more accepted. When I got out of prison in 1961 I wrote to Tito to say to him perhaps it is understandable we argue about opinions about the government but I wish that personally there is no bitterness. He gave no answer to me.

I take no money from my publisher in America. This is because these ideas are required for advancement of society. About my wife I feel so happy to have this woman I cannot tell you. She has been very, very good. I told her one morning after I am sent to jail the second time get divorced from me for your good. She thinks about this for a while and refuses absolutely. I could never want more in my life than such a person as this. This is why now I am very happy.

FIVE

THE RUSSIANS

On August twenty-first they invaded Czechoslovakia. Germans, Poles, Hungarians and Bulgarians entered Czechoslovakia with them at eighteen points in the north, northwest, south and east. A division of their infantrymen landed at Ruzyne Airport near Prague in two hundred and fifty airplanes. The Czechoslovakian army was ordered not to resist the invasion by their army. Their soldiers occupied strategic cities and captured government buildings. Their soldiers fired at buildings and at several civilians. They captured Premier Cernik at three o'clock in the morning at the Straca Military Academy. They captured First Secretary Dubcek and President of the National Assembly Smrkovsky at four o'clock in the morning at the building of the Central Committee. They took the First Secretary, the President of the National Assembly and the Premier to a barn near Sliac in Slovakia. They gave them little food and mistreated them. Their tanks broke through barricades surrounding the building of the Prague Radio on Vinohradska Street. Delegates to a congress of the Communist Party met in secret to resist their attempts to establish a puppet government. Their tanks surrounded Hradcany Castle and did not permit President Svoboda to leave it. They took First Secretary Dubcek and the others to Lvov in the Ukraine. They took President Svoboda to Moscow. They took the First Secretary and the others to Moscow and forced the First Secretary, the President and the others to sign a treaty providing that two of their army divisions be permanently stationed in Czechoslovakia on the German border.

A troupe of their entertainers from Moscow sang and danced in the Vrchlickeho Park opposite the main railway station. Two thousand of their soldiers were bivouacked near tanks and armored personnel carriers in the park. The entertainers danced Cossack dances, sang Russian folk songs and recited. The entertainers sang the British song "Happy Neighbors." Two of the entertainers were pretty young girls. Their soldiers clapped and cheered. Their soldiers stood at their ease with their automatic rifles slung muzzle downwards. Some of the soldiers joined in the dancing. A few Czechoslovaks watched the entertainers perform. A young man wearing a button watched. The button read "I Love You" in English. Several young couples and young girls stood watching among the soldiers. An American watched from over the shoulders of several soldiers. The soldiers invited him to watch from in front of them and made room for him. Children played on seesaws and swings among their soldiers. Some of their officers watched from a distance. A major speaking fluent English expressed surprise an American told him he was enjoying the performance. After an hour and a half the entertainers finished their performance. The last dance was a fast march. The entertainers executed it with their eyes fixed on red flags they waved at each end of the line of dancers. Some of their soldiers gathered around the young girls who had been watching the entertainers. A young lieutenant from Leningrad talked with a pretty English girl in good English. He said he had learned English in school. He asked the English girl what East European films she had recently attended and said of English-language films he preferred cowboy films. He asked the English girl about the fashion styles in London and said he thought English women all wore pointed shoes with spiked heals but the English girl told him flat shoes were all the vogue. The English girl walked past a group of their soldiers sitting on the grass. One of the soldiers played the guitar and another wrote a letter. "They all seem so young and so homesick," she said. She asked to take the soldiers' photograph and the soldiers gave their permission when she agreed that she would sit and talk with them afterwards.

An Englishman talked with one of their officers. "I imagine you'd find a very respectable audience for that sort of show at the Royal Albert," he said. "Without the tanks, of course." The officer scowled angrily at the Englishman and refused to speak further with him. "It's rather a pity to have to say so," the Englishman said later, "but the truth is they are a people that're after being a bit too touchy."

GENERAL G.

General G. stood stiffly. General G. stood in the Crematory Hall in Moscow. He stood beside an open coffin. Three hundred mourners stood near the coffin. An American newspaper reporter and an English newspaper reporter stood near the coffin.

"I ask, who is responsible for his death?" said General G. "Is it not the betrayers, the false colleagues who would pretend to be his friends and turn on him before he knew it? It is a great sadness to be betrayed. It is possible to die of sadness.

"Our friend Alyoshka did not rest, never. Until the very last day he struggled against corruption of power. We will never stop in this fight. The enemies of Alyoshka are our enemies. We will not stop until they are brought to account and recant what they have done.

"Who are the enemies of Alyoshka? Who did Alyoshka despise? Everyone who takes the words of Lenin and turns them inside out. Everyone who understands democracy to be telling men what they must do without anyone questioning or thinking. Everyone who becomes a wheel of the machine of bureaucrats who does not make himself squeak loudly, who does not raise his voice and protest.

"What am I to say of those in the Writers' Union who expelled him last month? That they have only brought shame to themselves? Did it never occur to them that they were not capable of removing a man from the ranks of writer? They forget that neither Pushkin nor Tolstoy was a member of the Union of Soviet Writers, and Pasternak was expelled.

"They wanted to expel Solzhenitsyn, when it is Solzhenitsyn who conferred honor on the Union of Writers by being its member and the Union confers nothing on Solzhenitsyn. Do they not understand that it is more honorable for any real writer to share the fate of Pasternak than to sit in meetings alongside the Voronkovs and the Ilyins?

"Alyoshka has been first, we have followed. He has created me. He has turned a mutineer into a fighter.

"What has happened? Why is it necessary for us who have been communists for forty years to become fighters? It is simple. The authorities do not respect man.

"A man, in Alyoshka's idea, is a thinking being. Therefore nature has given to him a striving for knowledge, so it is possible for him to critically evaluate reality, drawing one's own conclusions and freely stating one's convictions and opinions.

"For this he was terribly hated by those who believe that people exist to create a backdrop for 'leaders,' to applaud and shout 'hurrah' for them, to believe in them blindly, to pray for them, to endure without murmur all scorn of themselves and to quack with pleasure when into his trough they pour more fodder and richer fodder than into the other troughs.

"Alyoshka said to me all the time it is his greatest hope that such people will not dominate mankind forever. This is our hope also.

"He hated not only them but also the order they had created. He tirelessly repeated Lenin's words, 'There is nothing harsher and more soulless than a bureaucratic machine.' Therefore he believed that a communist has no higher task than to destroy this machine."

Afterwards the American newspaper reporter wrote in his newspaper that General G. had spoken eloquently over the body of his friend, the writer Aleksei K. Afterwards the American reporter wrote that Aleksei K. had been a member of the Communist Party for fifty-two years and had died four days before at the age of seventy-two. The American reporter wrote that the month before Aleksei K. had been expelled from the Party and had been expelled without his knowledge from the Union of Soviet Writers on account of his repeated charges that Stalinism was again gaining ascendency in the Soviet Union.

The American reporter wrote that in a country where politics was the concern of the secretive few and the voice of the great public was heard only as the "stormy applause" in newspaper accounts of the speeches of the few, it was very rare to hear an individual note of political discord. An individual voice speaking publicly and insistently, speaking words of radical opposition to the offical voices, was virtually a miracle. The American reporter wrote that such a voice had been raised at the cremation of Aleksei K. and had been raised louder than ever.

The American reporter wrote that it was the voice of Pyotr G. It was the voice, Pyotr G.'s friends said, of the conscience of the Soviet nation of two hundred and thirty-six million people. His friends were few. Because his friends were few Pyotr G. was reviled not only by the officials and the bureaucrats but this did not appear to pain him. The American reporter wrote that on the occasions when he had spoken his mind to those who were not his friends Pyotr G. had felt the hatred, the contempt or the indifference of the ordinary Soviet citizen.

The American reporter wrote that before and during the brief ceremony before the cremation of Aleksei K. attendants at the Crematory Hall had angrily declared to the mourners that no long ritual was permitted. General G. had been interrupted in his ten-minute speech by urgings over the public address system that his time was up. General G. had looked up angrily and hurried his speech as much as he could while he had struggled to keep his voice under control and his voice had gotten smaller and had sometimes broken with sorrow and anger. The American reporter wrote that General G. had also been harassed by a woman who had kept telling him to get it over with and had been badgered by a minor official of a literary welfare organization who had declared that the ceremony was prolonging itself beyond the proper time.

The American reporter wrote that General G. had not satisfied himself with praising in public the nearly forbidden names of Pasternak and Solzhenitsyn but also had praised as heroes the victims of recent Soviet trials of dissident intellectuals, who General G. declared were friends of Mr. Aleksei K. General G. had praised Yuri T. Galanskov and Aleksandr Ginzburg, who had been sentenced to prison camps the previous January, Vladimir I. Bukovsky, who had been sentenced the previous year, and others who General G. said he could not name for understandable reasons.

The American reporter wrote that even if the general had not named them, it was probable that they had been in the bleak, vaulted Crematory Hall, because most of the intense and sensitive faces of the solitary groups of Moscow's dissidents, who were normally seen only outside courthouses when their comrades were on trial, had seemed to be in the hall. The American reporter wrote that General G. himself was a familiar figure at the rare demonstrations of dissidence in the Soviet Union. The American reporter wrote that also in the hall had been a number of agents of the secret police bureaus that kept the dissidents under surveillance.

The American reporter wrote that a new element that had swelled the group of mourners above the usual number of dissidents were representatives of various national minorities, especially Crimean Tatars. The American reporter wrote that Aleksei K. had made his own the cause of minorities persecuted by Stalin and never fully rehabilitated.

The American reporter wrote that earlier, at the morgue in the Botkin Hospital, a brief ceremony attended by the same friends had been interrupted when attendants had moved another open coffin among the mourners and had begun to negotiate with a sobbing relative the bureaucratic details of signing over the body for the funeral. This had interrupted the reading of a tribute to the writer Aleksei K. by the poet Anatoly Y.

The American reporter wrote that a woman attendant had also interrupted Anatoly Y. when she had announced above Anatoly Y.'s speech that the time was up and the morgue was closing. The mourners had quickly gathered up the wreaths they had brought.

The American reporter wrote that the ribbon on one wreath had read "For his struggle against Stalinism." Another ribbon had read "From his comrades in the prisons and camps." Aleksei K. had spent seventeen years in Stalin's prison camps. Another ribbon had read. "To the father of Nina, from readers." Aleksei K. was best known for his daughter, who had been killed on a partisan mission behind German lines at the age of twenty and whose diary had been published in 1962 and had been widely read.

The American reporter wrote that General G. had also been subjected to the same public scorn and contempt the month before when he had held vigil outside a courthouse for five of his friends who had been standing trial for publicly protesting the invasion of Czechoslovakia. In the street the dissidents had argued with the plainclothesmen of the secret police who followed them wherever they went, and with the zealous party members who are detailed to represent "public opinion" on such occasions. The American reporter wrote that these people had tried by every means to provoke the old officer, who had stood straight as a ramrod in the hostile crowd, asking him questions in tones of contempt and sending him drinks to rattle his composure.

The American reporter wrote that General G. had remained patient and had never seemed to lose his sense of humor. He had talked seriously about how, in his opinion, Lenin's thought has been perverted by his successors, and had answered gibes with jokes. The American reporter wrote that for a man so single-minded and so endowed with a sense of mission, the broad-shouldered Ukrainian, who looked very much like a rustic character from a Russian novel of the last century, was remarkable for his good temper and the easy smile that lighted his pale blue Slavic eyes.

The American reporter wrote that General G.'s single-mindedness concerning the rule of law and his hatred of the arbitrary exercise of power had carried him into quixotic situations and made some people consider him an inspired madman. The American reporter wrote that such a situation had occurred in front of the courthouse the month before. A man who had appeared plainly to be a member of the secret police had torn a petition protesting the refusal of the court attendants to allow friends of the defendants into the courtroom. General G. had barked at the presumed agent that this was hooliganism and had swung his walking stick menacingly. General G. had demanded that the young man identify himself so that he could be reported. The American reporter wrote that a police officer among the crowd had been startled by this insubordination in a country where people commonly argued with uniformed police but where everyone submitted to agents in civilian clothes and had told both of them to go to the nearest police station. The American reporter wrote that the result in the station had been inconclusive but those who had witnessed the incident asked who but a madman would have marched a secret police agent to the nearest police station to file a complaint against him?

The American reporter wrote that General G. had joined the Communist Party forty-one years before at the age of twenty and had held degrees in military science and engineering, had joined the army in 1930 and had fought against the Japanese in the Mongolian border incident in May 1939. In World War II General G. had held high command positions, becoming a major general, had been wounded twice and had been frequently decorated, and subsequently had taught at the Frunze Military Academy in Moscow.

The American reporter wrote that General G. had lost his position at the military academy in 1961 when he made a bold speech at a party meeting in which he warned that Premier Khrushchev was establishing a regime based on the cult of personality, a politic way of saying that Khrushchev was acting like Stalin. General G. had been given a minor post in the Far East. The American reporter wrote that General G. had written about himself that not frightened by this repression he had begun a systematic struggle against all forms of arbitrariness.

The American reporter wrote that General G. had bean arrested in February 1964 and had spent seven months in prison without a trial, and eight more months in a prison psychiatric ward, a common place of detention for dissidents in the Soviet Union. General G. had been freed after Khrushchev was ousted from power in October 1964, but had bean reduced from major general to private and discharged from the army without pension.

The American reporter wrote that General G. had also been expelled from the Party on the charge of insanity, an action which had not been revoked when he had been certified sane in 1965. The American reporter wrote that since his liberation from the Party the general's dissidence, which had been kept within Party circles until then, had become public. No protest, whether against the suppression of literary works or the jailing of writers, discrimination against national minorities or the invasion of Czechoslovakia, appeared complete without his signature or presence.

The American reporter wrote that after joining in sending a letter the previous February to a world communist conference protesting against "the trampling on man" in the Soviet Union, General G. had lost his job as a construction foreman. Since than he had been unable to find work other than as a common laborer.

The American reporter wrote that the general's wife, Zinaida, whose first husband had been killed by Stalinist persecution, was also a long-time member of the Party and shared her husband's opinions.

Afterwards the American reporter wrote that since the earliest years of the Soviet state it was doubtful that so open and radical an opposition speech had been publicly delivered. Afterwards the American reporter wrote that General G. had stood over the open coffin of his comrade and denounced "the totalitarianism that hides behind the mask of so-called Soviet democracy."

"In farewells it is usually said, 'Sleep quietly, Dear Comrade," said General G. in the Crematory Hall. "We shall not say this. In the first place, he will not listen to me. He will continue to fight anyway.

"In the second place, it is impossible for me without you, Alyoshka. You are inside me and you will remain there. Without you, I do not live. Therefore do not sleep, Alyoshka! Fight, Alyoshka!

"Destroy all the abominable meanness with which they want to keep turning eternally the damned machine against which you fought all your life. We, your friends, will not be far behind you.

"Freedom will come! Democracy will come!"

A woman played Chopin's Funeral March on an organ in the Crematory Hall. General G. stood stiffly, listening to the Funeral March. A woman wearing a black smock declared that she was now to nail the lid on the coffin. The mourners prevented the woman from nailing the lid on the coffin immediately. Several of the mourners kissed the forehead of the corpse. The woman nailed the lid on the coffin. The coffin was lowered into a trap. A woman turned off the lights in the hall and told the mourners to leave quickly.

A week after the speech of General G. in the Crematory Hall the English reporter said to the American reporter he had invited General G. to dine with him that night to meet General G. The English reporter asked the American reporter if he wished to dine with him and General G. to meet General G.

The American reporter said he did not wish to dine with them. The American reporter said he was dining at the Metropole Hotel that night. He was dining with a woman friend. The woman friend was a Frenchwoman and was visiting in Moscow.

The English reporter suggested that the four of them might dine together at the Metropole Hotel.

"I'd really rather not," said the American reporter. "I really don't think he's exactly the kind of person Nan would like to see. I thought I might introduce her to the director of the Art Theater or someone like that while she's here. Besides, with Nan there and at the Metropole and all I'd be a little afraid what he might do. I mean, after all, he *is* more than just a little bit crazy."

SIX

THE ATHEIST

He was an atheist. He disliked religion. He said all religion was repugnant to him. He said God should not be in government. He said he wanted to get God out of the government. In the nineteen twenties and thirties he campaigned for the separation of church and state. He campaigned for the institution of elections on Sundays. He campaigned for the institution of mail deliveries on Sundays. He campaigned against released time for religious instruction in public schools. He campaigned against the transportation of crippled children to parochial schools at public expense. He instituted a suit to prevent the New York City government from using the money of the Welfare Department to transport crippled children to parochial schools. He campaigned for the deletion of the phrase "under God" from the Pledge of Allegiance. He instituted a suit to delete the phrase "under God" from the Pledge of Allegiance. The suit contended that the phrase "under God" was proscribed by the First Amendment to the Constitution. The suit was heard before the United States Supreme Court. The United States Supreme Court ruled that the phrase "under God" in the Pledge of Allegiance was not proscribed by the First Amendment to the Constitution.

He was Nathan Joseph. He was born on June 11, 1889. He was born in Montgomery, Alabama. He was the son of a Jewish merchant. He had never been religious. "I abandoned the notions of religion early in life," he said. He lived in Miami Beach. In 1920 he founded the Atheists Society of America. He was president of the Atheists Society of America.

In 1925 he moved to New York State. He lived in a house in Purdys, New York. He gave a great many speeches on the subject of atheism. He wrote a great many books on the subject of atheism. He owned the Freethinker Press publishing company. The offices of the Freethinker Press publishing company were at 959 West Thirty-Eighth Street. He admired Thomas Paine. He wrote biographies of Thomas Paine. He was president of the Thomas Paine Association. He believed that Thomas Paine wrote the Declaration of Independence. In 1947 he wrote a book which he declared proved that Thomas Paine wrote the Declaration of Independence.

He said he was an infidel. He believed that the intelligence of man had increased during the twentieth century. He believed that the intelligence of men had increased to the extent that men were throwing off the dead hand of religious superstition. He believed that men were now realizing that man's salvation lies with his fellow man alone. "An atheist cannot be mentioned in the same breath with that impulse and conviction which produces religious mania, religious strife, religious hatred, religious prejudice. Religious love is clannish. Christian loves Christian and Jew loves Jew. Atheists love everybody. They are lovers of mankind," he said.

He campaigned to prevent the closing of schools for Rosh Hashanah and Yom Kippur. He urged Jews to renounce their religion. He declared that the Jewish religion was an antiquated creed. He denounced Yom Kippur. He declared that Yom Kippur was the most degrading and humiliating day in all the superstitious annals of religion. Six honorary vice-presidents of the Atheists Society of America resigned in protest when he denounced Yom Kippur. He campaigned to prevent the building of Protestant, Jewish and Roman Catholic chapels at the Kennedy Airport. He campaigned against the presence of chaplains in the armed forces, the police department, the fire department and the houses of Congress. He denounced Thanksgiving. He declared that Thanksgiving was hypocritical and childish and weighted with religious significance. He denounced public celebration of Christmas. In 1962 he campaigned to prevent the Post Office Department from issuing a Christmas stamp. In 1929 he denounced

President Herbert Hoover. "Herbert Hoover's first act after taking the oath of office as President in kissing the Bible was a most unbecoming and stupid act," he said. He complained to an aide of President Herbert Hoover. The aide of President Herbert Hoover listened to his complaint. The aide of President Herbert Hoover laughed.

He wrote "Freethinkers Manifesto." He wrote "The Slavery of Religion." He wrote "The Crime against Mankind." In "The Crime against Mankind" he denounced circumcision. He declared that circumcision was a harmful practice that was a legacy of superstitious religious customs and had no medical value. He wrote "The Serpents of God." He declared that "The Serpents of God" exposed the seamy side of the lives of religious heroes. He wrote "The Bible Revealed." In "The Bible Revealed" he cited certain passages of the Bible. He declared that the passages of the Bible he cited were pornographic.

He wrote a great many letters to newspapers. He wrote letters to newspapers on the subject of atheism. He denounced faults in the collection of garbage in New York. He denounced faults in the street lighting in New York. He denounced excessive noise in New York. He denounced the chimes in the tower of the Metropolitan Life Insurance Company building.

He wrote "The Fable of Christianity." "The Fable of Christianity" was published after he died. He died on November 5, 1968. He died in the offices of the Freethinker Press on West Thirty-Eighth Street. He went to the offices of the Freethinker Press at ten o'clock in the morning and died at his desk. He suffered a heart attack and died.

His associates said he had been a jolly man. His associates said he had been a good-natured man. His associates said he had been very energetic despite his age. He was survived by his wife. His wife was Sara Hendel Sollinger. He was survived by his daughter and grandson. He was survived by his sister. His sister was Mrs. Sadie Newman. He had not wanted a funeral to be held for him. He had prohibited a funeral from being held for him in his will. He had denounced funerals in his will. He had declared in his will that funerals were obsolete rituals intended to perpetuate religious superstitions. His sister wanted a funeral to be *held for him. His sister said it would be unthinkable for a funeral not to be held for him. A funeral was held for him. The funeral was held at the Riverside Funeral Chapel. The Riverside Funeral Chapel was at Seventy-Sixth Street and Amsterdam Avenue. A large number of people attended the funeral.*

His sister was pleased that a funeral had been held for him although he had prohibited a funeral from being held for him. His sister was pleased with his funeral. His sister wept after the funeral. "Bless us, such a beautiful funeral," she said.

THE MODERN ARTIST

He was a modern artist. He was a very famous modern artist. He was rich. He was old. He was very old. He was eighty-one years old. One day he died. He died in his studio in the Paris suburb of Neuilly one day. He died after having eaten dinner with his wife and some friends. He collapsed and died. He ate fried chicken at dinner and collapsed and died. Critics wrote that his death was paradoxical.

Before he died he believed eating the fried chicken had caused him to collapse. Before he died he believed that something he ate had caused him to collapse. He said he shouldn't have eaten the fried chicken. He said he wouldn't have eaten the fried chicken if he had known the fried chicken would cause him to collapse. He said he didn't want to die. He said he was afraid to die. He said he hoped he wouldn't discover that hell existed after all. He said he wouldn't like to go to hell. Critics wrote that what he said before he died was paradoxical. Critics wrote that what he said before he died was paradoxical and conventional. It was paradoxical that what he said was conventional. He was unconventional. Critics wrote that he was being ironically paradoxical in the conventional things he said before he died.

Critics wrote that he was a paradoxical artist. Critics wrote that he had a paradoxical personality. Critics wrote that paradox was a dominant recessive in modern art. Critics wrote that paradox was embodied in his career and life. Critics wrote that he acquired dignity by acting with impudence. Critics wrote that he achieved godhood by denying all the gods. Critics wrote that his abstention from creative endeavor made him a positive creative force. Critics wrote that his esthetic nihilism solidified a new esthetic. Critics wrote that he looked like a humanistic scholar. He might have been expected to be a humanistic scholar. He spoke like a humanistic scholar. Critics wrote that by any traditional humanistic standards he was a Beelzebub. Critics wrote that he was supposed to be the most world-weary of cynics. Critics wrote that he lived with as much gusto as a child. Critics wrote that he was an utterly charming man in spite of his having a paradoxical personality. He was born near Rouen. He was born in Blainville. Blainville is a village near Rouen.

"Blainville is a charming village near Rouen. It is very charming and very small. It is uninhabitable. It is much too idyllic," he said.

He was born on the twenty-eighth of July 1887. His father was a notary. His father was rich. He was his father's third son. He had two brothers. He had a sister. His brothers and sister were artists. Critics wrote that his brothers and sister were extremely gifted artists. Critics wrote that the older of his brothers, Gaston, was an extremely gifted artist who achieved international renown as a painter. The older of his brothers died. The older of his brothers died in 1963. Critics wrote that the younger of his brothers, Jacques, was an extremely gifted artist who was among the leading sculptors of his generation. The younger of his brothers died. The younger of his brothers died in the First World War. Critics wrote that his sister was an extremely gifted artist. His sister was a painter. His sister died.

"Of course with everyone else in my family becoming artists it was unthinkable for me to think of becoming an artist. So of course I became an artist," he said.

His parents approved of his studying to become an artist. He studied to become an artist. He left home with his parents' approval when he was seventeen and studied to become an artist at the Academie Julian in Paris. He lived in Paris in quarters with his brother Jacques and studied to become an artist. Critics wrote that he arrived in Paris at the twilight of an epoch. Critics wrote that in a few years Braque and Picasso were to shatter the conventions of representational art with Cubism. Critics wrote that soon Futurism would compete with Cubism for the attentions of the avant garde. Critics wrote that soon Dada would proclaim the destruction of established values. Critics wrote that the search for new forms and the achievement of so many new forms followed the upheaval of the First World War and the destruction of the old order. He did not like studying to become an artist at the Academie Julian. He was dissatisfied with the Academie Julian.

"I was already disgusted with the cuisine of painting. I mostly played billiards at this time," he said.

He became a soldier. He was a soldier in the army for a year. He disliked being a soldier. Critics wrote that he demonstrated an easy technical grasp of Cezanne and Matisse. Critics wrote that he began to experiment with the geometry and muted colors of Cubism. Critics wrote that his brothers adapted their sensibilities to Cubism but that he began to alter his style. Critics wrote that like the Futurists he began to employ a succession of flat overlapping planes to depict spatial movement of machine-like forms. Critics wrote that he supplemented his work with verbal extra-visual ideas. Critics wrote that the idea of his famous "Nude Walking Mechanical Woman" had first been expressed in a poem. Critics wrote that the painting with which he was most associated was "Nude Walking Mechanical Woman." "Nude Walking Mechanical Woman" was a famous painting. Critics wrote that "Nude Walking Mechanical Woman" was one of the most famous paintings of modern art. "Nude Walking Mechanical Woman" hung in the Arensberg Collection of the Philadelphia Museum of Art. Critics wrote that "Nude Walking Mechanical Woman" was worth more than two hundred and fifty thousand dollars.

In 1912 he made preliminary studies for "Nude Walking Mechanical Woman." In 1912 he submitted "Nude Walking Mechanical Woman" to the exhibition of the Puteaux circle at the Salon de Independents. Critics wrote that the Futurist elements of "Nude Walking Mechanical Woman" angered members of the Puteaux circle. Members of the Puteaux circle asked him to withdraw "Nude Walking Mechanical Woman" from the exhibition. His brothers asked him to withdraw "Nude Walking Mechanical Woman."

"I put the painting under my arm, got into a taxi and went home. After that circles or groups meant very little to me," he said. In 1915 he exhibited "Nude Walking Mechanical Woman" in New York. He exhibited "Nude Walking Mechanical Woman" in the Armory Show. The Armory Show was at the Sixty-Ninth Regiment Armory at Twenty-Fifth Street and Lexington Avenue in New York. Critics wrote that the Armory Show in New York in 1915 was the most famous exhibition that has ever been given in America. Critics wrote that the Armory Show in New York created a sensation.

Critics wrote that the organizers of the Armory Show, the Association of American Painters and Sculptors, anticipated the clamor that America's first exposure to Europe's new nonrepresentational painting would generate. Critics wrote that the organizers created a circus atmosphere for the inspection of the new art. Critics wrote that the organizers deluged newspapers with press releases and newspapers drew satirical cartoons and wrote derisive commentary. Critics wrote that newspapers wrote that "Nude Walking Mechanical Woman" looked like a painting of an explosion in a shingle factory and a collection of saddlebags.

Critics wrote that the public was outraged at the Cubist paintings in the exhibition. Critics wrote that the Armory Show turned many Americans into art critics. Critics wrote that the Armory Show turned President Theodore Roosevelt into an art critic. Critics wrote that President Theodore Roosevelt criticized the Cubist paintings in the exhibition. Critics wrote that President Theodore Roosevelt said, "There is no reason why people should not call themselves Cubists or knights of the isosceles triangle. One term is as fatuous as another." Critic's wrote that large crowds of people attended the Armory Show and guards had to restrain outraged art lovers from damaging the paintings. Critics wrote that "Nude Walking Mechanical Woman" is an organization of kinetic elements, an expression of time and space through the abstract presentation of motion.

"A painting is, of necessity, a juxtaposition of two or more colors on a surface. I purposely restricted the 'Nude' to wood coloring so that the question of painting per se might not be raised.

"In considering the motion of form through space in a given time it is necessary to enter the realm of geometry and mathematics.

"If I show the ascent of an airplane, I try to show what it does. I do not make a still-life picture of it. When the vision of the 'Nude' flashed upon me I knew that it would break forever the enslaving chains of naturalism," he said.

Critics wrote that the reaction of the public to "Nude Walking Mechanical Woman" was outrage. Critics wrote that the outraged reaction of the public to "Nude Walking

Mechanical Woman" made his name a household word. "I found it very pleasant because after all my aim was not to please the general public. The scandal was exactly in my program, you might say. Also I received two hundred and forty dollars. That also was very pleasant," he said.

He knew Francis Picabia. He was a friend of Francis Picabia. Critics wrote that he and Francis Picabia each had an iconoclastic wit and an absurd sense of humor. Critics wrote that he and Francis Picabia knew other men having an iconoclastic wit and an absurd sense of humor. He and Francis Picabia knew Alfred Jarry. Critics wrote that Alfred Jarry had an iconoclastic wit and an absurd sense of humor. Critics wrote that Alfred Jarry suffered from malnutrition and on his deathbed asked for a toothpick. He and Francis Picabia knew Eric Satie. Critics wrote that Eric Satie had an iconoclastic wit and an absurd sense of humor. Critics wrote that Eric Satie's music had been criticized as being formless and Eric Satie named a musical work he wrote "Three Pieces in the Form of a Pear."

Critics wrote that he began to question the visual basis of art. Critics wrote that art had a visual basis.

"I wanted to get away from the physical aspects of painting. I was interested in ideas, not merely in visual products. I wanted to put painting again in the service of the mind," he said.

Critics wrote that he developed a playful physics. Critics wrote that he found scientific laws to be too arbitrary. Critics wrote that he formulated his own scientific laws.

"Why must we worship principles which in fifty or a hundred years will no longer apply?" he said.

Critics wrote he devised a personal logic in which cause and effect became subject to chance. Critics wrote that according to his personal logic an apple might not choose to obey the law of gravity and love-making might exist as a fourth-dimensional ritual of machines and a real safety pin might hold together a tear painted on a canvas. Critics wrote that he was dissatisfied with the meter as a unit of measurement. Critics wrote that he created his own unit of measurement. He cut pieces of thread one meter long and dropped the thread on painted canvas. He dropped the threads on the painted canvas from a height of one meter. He covered the threads with varnish. He made wooden rulers from the canvas and threads. "It was these rulers which later I used in drawing lines on transparent glass to compose my monumental unfinished 'The Beautiful Young Woman in Disdress and Partial Recovery' or 'The Big Glass,' as I sometimes called it," he said.

Critics wrote that he painted witty and absurd paintings, He painted "Nude Dressed for Dinner." "Nude Dressed for Dinner" was a painting of a woman wearing only a shirt front and cuffs. He painted "Puddles in Pavement." "Puddles in Pavement" was a painting of three small flasks filled with water.

He invented ready-mades. In 1913 he began making ready-mades. Critics wrote that ready-mades were everyday objects which he elevated by mere selection to the stature of art. Critics wrote that his paradoxical and parodistic gestures against retinal art were the beginning of pop and junk sculptures.

"In New York in 1915 I bought at a hardware store a snow shovel on which I wrote 'in advance of a broken arm.'

"It was around that time that the word 'ready-made' came to my mind to designate this form of manifestation.

"A point that I want very much to establish is that the choice of these ready-mades was never dictated by esthetic delectation. The choice was based on a reaction of visual

97

indifference with a total absence of good or bad taste, in fact a complete anesthesia.

"Sometimes I would add a graphic detail of presentation which, in order to satisfy my craving for alliterations, would be called 'ready-made aided.'

"At another time I wanted to expose the basic antinomy between art and ready-mades. I imagined a reciprocal ready-made: a Rembrandt used as an ironing board," he said.

He did not fight in the First World War. He was not a soldier in the army during the First World War. He had a heart ailment. Critics wrote that he became a target of abuse in the midst of the patriotic fervor of the first World War. Critics wrote that he shunned Parisian cafe life almost entirely. Critics wrote that he was never drawn by the spectacle of Parisian cafe life. In 1915 he went to New York. It was the first time he had gone to New York. Critics wrote that he was a celebrity in New York. He was a celebrity on account of the scandal he had created by exhibiting "Nude Walking Mechanical Woman" in the Armory Show. Critics wrote that he was less reserved in New York than he was in Paris. Critics wrote that he quickly fell into an avant garde artistic circle and a glittering social milieu. Critics wrote that people found his conversation witty and his manner elegant. Critics wrote that women found his gray eyes, reddish-blond hair and sharply-defined features very masculine. "There is art and there are women. Art is more necessary but women are more pleasant," he said.

In 1917 he resigned from the Society of Independent Artists. He complained about the Society of Independent Artists. The Society of Independent Artists abandoned its policy of accepting for exhibition any work for which the artist paid a fee of six dollars. The Society of Independent Artists refused to exhibit a work. The Society of Independent Artists refused to exhibit an inverted urinal. The title of the inverted urinal was "Fountain." The inverted urinal was signed with the name R. Fish of Philadelphia. He argued that the inverted urinal ought to be permitted to be exhibited. He had submitted the inverted urinal for exhibition under the name R. Fish. He said it was intolerable that the Society of Independent Artists refused to exhibit the inverted urinal. "I said there was no good reason why this sculpture should not be shown to the public. I believed it is a very thoughtful apparatus for the study of hydrodynamics," he said.

Critics wrote that he made witty sculptures. He made the sculpture "Trust in God." "Trust in God" was a sculpture of a man wearing an athletic support. He made the sculpture "Portrait of Mummy." "Portrait of Mummy" was a sculpture of a figure wrapped in a canvas on which a portrait of an old woman was painted. He made "Painting of Explosion." "Painting of Explosion" was a heap of shreds of canvas.

He visited Paris. In 1919 he visited Paris. Critics wrote that in 1919 Dada was in full bloom in Paris. Critics wrote that he was the hero of the Dada movement. He contributed a painting to Francis Picabia's *591* magazine. The painting was a copy of the "Mona Lisa" on which he had drawn a moustache and goatee. The name of the painting was "Ready-Made Aided Mona Lisa." He returned to New York. Critics wrote that he returned to New York without taking part in the organized Dada activities. Critics wrote that returning to New York without taking part in the organized Dada activities enhanced his prestige.

In Paris he made the collage "Venal Eye Catcher." "Venal Eye Catcher" was a collage depicting Venus. The collage consisted of dollar bills covered with a sticky substance. He painted "April in Paris." "April in Paris" was a painting of a French calendar of the month of April. He painted "The Flying Machine." "The Flying Machine" was a painting of a lathe having wings. He painted "Artist at Work." "Artist at Work" was a painting of a man digging with a pick. He painted

"Diving Bell." "Diving Bell" was a painting of a diver inside a diving bell. The diver inside the diving bell had cotton in his ears. He painted "Ash Tray." "Ash Tray" was a painting of an ashtray. There were images of cigarette burns painted on the canvas of the painting. He painted "Automobile." "Automobile" was a painting depicting phallic shapes. He painted "Assumption." "Assumption" was a copy of a painting of the Assumption of the Virgin. The painting was exhibited hung on a grappling hook.

"All the time I strived for wit as relief from perfection in art. I believed perfection in art to be tedious and unsatisfying and to be avoided whenever possible," he said.

He said he no longer desired to paint on canvas. He abandoned painting on canvas. He said painting on canvas was to difficult. He said in painting on canvas it was too difficult avoiding the praise of the public. He adopted a false name. He adopted the name Rose Sélavy. Rose Sélavy was a pun. Rose Sélavy was a pun on the words "C'est la vie." He began to assemble "The Beautiful Young Woman in Disdress and Partial Recovery." He believed "The Beautiful Young Woman in Disdress and Partial Recovery" would be an important work. He believed "The Beautiful Young Woman in Distress and Partial Recovery" would be his masterpiece. He made "Fresh Widow." "Fresh Widow" was a carpenter's model of a French window. The panes of the model French window were covered with black leather. He made "Still Life with Bread and Wine." "Still Life with Bread and Wine" was an aquarium filled with wine in which a wine bottle was submerged. In the wine bottle was a piece of bread. He made "Painting of Gallery with Painting of Gallery." "Painting of Gallery with Painting of Gallery" was an empty picture frame. The empty picture frame was hung from wires in the center of galleries. He made destructions. Destructions were sculptures made from fragments of copies of famous sculptures.

"Others called their sculptures constructions. I called certain of my sculptures destructions because I produced new combinations through the destruction of dead esthetics of the past. I believed my destructions were in reality creations. They were destructions of the baggage of art and creations, of ideas," he said.

He wrote poems. He wrote the poem "Verses without Rhyme or Reason." "Verses without Rhyme or Reason" consisted of excerpts from newspaper and magazine notices. The notices were newspaper and magazine notices critics had written about his work. He wrote a play. He wrote "Mirror Play." He wrote "Mirror Play" by reversing the order of the lines of a nineteenth century melodrama.

"By taking a very bad play and having it acted backwards I hoped to achieve a reversal of values and create a masterpiece," he said.

He worked on "The Beautiful Young Woman in Disdress and Partial Recovery." He worked on "The Beautiful Young Woman and Partial Recovery" for eight years. He did not like to work steadily. He did not work for more than a few hours at a time. In 1925 he stopped working on "The Beautiful Young Woman in Disdress and Partial Recovery."

"The whole thing no longer interested me," he said.

Critics wrote that in 1925 he made his departure from the formal practice of art. He disapproved of the commercialization of art and the acceptance of art by the middle class. He played chess. He spent a good deal of time playing chess. He enjoyed playing chess after he abandoned painting and sculpture. He had always enjoyed playing chess. He had enjoyed playing chess since he was a young man. Critics wrote that while he was not of master caliber chess experts considered him a good match. Critics wrote that he would rather risk losing by playing an unusual game than win by playing a conventional game. Critics wrote that during the nineteen-thirties and nineteen-forties he did not engage in public activity. He was an advisor of art dealers and collectors. Critics wrote that when he was asked if the legend was true that he had abandoned painting and sculpture to play chess he nodded in polite acquiescence. "My occupation? I am a respirateur," he said.

Critics wrote that unlike other exponents of Dada he did not become a conventional artist after the First World War and assimilate subsequent artistic developments. Critics wrote that in abandoning the creation of works of art he carried the vaudeville of esthetic nihilism to its logical conclusion. Critics wrote that his final exit from artistic creation was the perfect complement to his output as an artist. Critics wrote that for this reason his life as well as career was looked upon as having esthetic significance. Critics wrote that some critics regarded his withdrawal as an escape from his inadequacies as an artist. Critics wrote that he maintained an aristocratic detachment and reserve in the face of such speculations. Critics wrote that his abdication commanded the esteem of the avant garde. Critics wrote that he was the Duke of Windsor of modern art.

"I'm afraid I'm an agnostic in art. I just don't believe in art with all the mystical trimmings. As a drug, it's probably very useful for a number of people—very seductive—but as religion it's not even as good as God.

"It is disastrous for an artist to defend his art. Posterity has to decide, and even if it is wrong in every respect it has the advantage of coming into being.

"I wish I could live another hundred years. But perhaps it would be better to be dead. You see, I find it perfectly acceptable to contradict myself," he said.

Critics wrote that contradiction was an important part of the ideological and artistic universe he created. Critics wrote that he created his own ideological and artistic universe. Critics wrote that he was very seriously tongue-in-cheek. Critics wrote that he implied that art was a game, at best an amusing game. Critics wrote that in a sense he was the most destructive artist in history. Critics wrote that he was the most destructive artist in history in the sense that in his position as the unquestionable authority he denied the legitimacy for our century of the techniques and philosophies of four thousand years of art. Critics wrote that at the same time and for the same reason he exerted the greatest influence on the course of modern art of anyone except Picasso.

Critics wrote that he was only six years younger than Picasso but the six years and his being a Frenchman may have accounted for the fact that the irrational spectacle of the First World War turned him away from the rational processes of Cubism that continued to occupy Picasso. Critics wrote that the rational processes of Cubism continued to occupy Picasso. Critics wrote that he was led in the anarchic movement of Dada to deny to art the rational premises that had already been rejected by a world bent on destroying itself.

Critics wrote that he had great appeal to several generations of intellectuals who felt that science had stripped them of traditional values and left them spiritually bankrupt. Critics wrote that he did not offer a cure for the spiritual malaise but at least offered wit, absurdity and the humor of paradox as an anodyne. Critics wrote that his work pointed to concepts in art that would be articulated by generations to come. Critics wrote that the concepts articulated by generations to come were the reality of the three-dimensional object replacing illusionism, the self-effacement of the artist, and the object competing with and merging into its environment. Critics wrote that there was hardly a contemporary experimental art movement that cannot be traced down through the branches of its family tree to him as its generative patriarch. Critics wrote that contrary to convention he as an innovator became a prophet. Critics wrote that he had no intention of becoming a prophet and was heaped with honors not only in his own country but in countries around the world. Critics wrote that he was not a great master as Picasso was a great master among others in the continuum of past centuries. Critics wrote that the tradition he began could possibly replace the tradition of the great masters of past centuries.

Critics wrote that the appearance of pop art in the early nineteen-sixties stirred a renewal of interest in his work. Critics wrote that there were sharp parallels between his work and pop art. Critics wrote that in pop art the celebration of the Coke bottle and the Campbell soup can and other mundane objects were intended as genuine artistic statements. "When I discovered ready-mades I thought to discourage esthetics. In Neo-Dada they have taken my ready-mades and found esthetic beauty in them. I threw the bottle-rack and the urinal into their faces as a challenge and now they admire them for their esthetic beauty," he said. Museums exhibited his works. In 1963 the Passadena Art Museum gave a large retrospective exhibition of his works. It was the first large retrospective exhibition of his works. In 1966 the Tate Gallery gave a large retrospective exhibition of his works. Critics wrote that he was showered with new public acclaim. Critics wrote that he accepted the new acclaim of the public. Critics wrote that he accepted the new acclaim of the public although he did not especially value acclaim of the public. "Of course anyone who is able to create ideas will become famous. It cannot be helped. It is tiresome and also rather pleasing," he said. He died. He died one day in 1968. He died on October second 1968.

He requested that he be buried in Blainville near Rouen. He requested that his funeral be at the Blainville village church. He requested that he be buried on a hill beneath a chestnut tree. He requested that he be buried near the graves of his father and mother. He requested that a prayer be recited over his grave committing his soul to heaven.

Critics wrote that what he requested was conventional. Critics wrote that he was being ironical in the conventional things he requested. Critics wrote that he was unconventional. Critics wrote that he was being ironically witty in the conventional things he requested when he died. Critics wrote that he had an ironical wit. Critics wrote that in abandoning life he made a grand gesture that was the logical conclusion of his esthetic nihilism. Critics wrote that his death had esthetic significance. Critics wrote that his death was fitting. Critics wrote that death was a fitting end to his life.

SEVEN

THE SWEATER

There was a crowd of men standing at the corner of Broad Street and Wall Street. There were Stock Exchange clerks standing in front of the Stock Exchange Building. The Stock Exchange clerks wore beige jackets. There were brokers looking out the windows of the Stock Exchange Building. There was a crowd of men standing on the steps of the Subtreasury Building. There were bankers looking out the windows of the Morgan Guaranty Trust Company Building. There were men standing on the roofs of buildings. There were men standing on the roofs of cars. Men standing on the roofs of two cars crushed the roofs of the cars. The crowd of men blocked the traffic along Broad Street and Wall Street. There were men hanging onto lampposts. There were men hanging onto the statue of George Washington. There was a man hanging onto the buttonwood tree. There were five thousand men standing at the corner of Broad Street and Wall Street.

The crowd of men watched the exit of a subway station. The crowd of men watched the exit of the BMT Broad Street subway station. At one twenty-five a man in the crowd shouted. The crowd of men pushed closer to the exit of the subway station. The crowd of men watched the exit of the subway station. No one walked from the exit of the subway station. Men in the crowd muttered disappointedly. At one thirty-four a man in the crowd shouted. A girl walked from the exit of the subway station.

The crowd of men pushed close to the girl. Two policemen escorted the girl. The crowd of men cheered. Onlookers asked the girl for her *autograph. Photographers took photographs of the girl. The girl's name was Maxine Greenberg. The girl lived in Williamsburg in Brooklyn. The policemen escorted the girl away from the crowd of men to the building at 15 Broad Street. The policemen escorted the girl out the back door of the building at 15 Broad Street. The policemen escorted the girl to the Chemical New York Trust Company Building at 2 Broadway. The girl worked as an operator of IBM machines in the Chemical Bank New York Trust Company. The girl wore a yellow sweater and a red skirt. The girl's hips were shapely. The girl's waist was small. The girl's breasts were very large. The sweater was very tight.*

Afterwards four newspaper reporters interviewed the girl. A reporter asked the girl if she was surprised. The reporter said he supposed she was surprised when the policemen told her a crowd of five thousand men had gathered to watch her walk from the exit of the subway station to the Chemical Bank New York Trust Company Building.

"No, not really. A lot of guys have been collecting along the street the past couple weeks. I kind of got the idea. Of course all this I didn't expect exactly," said the girl.

The reporters listened to the girl. The reporters finished writing on their stenographic pads. The reporters smiled.

A reporter asked the girl what her bust measurement was.

"Forty-three without taking a breath," said the girl.

The reporters listened to the girl. The reporters finished writing on their stenographic pads. The reporters smiled.

A reporter asked the girl why she wore sweaters.

"For the sex appeal, what do you think? I figure if you got something to show off you might as well show it off," said the girl.

The reporters listened to the girl. The reporters finished writing on their stenographic pads. The reporters smiled. The reporters laughed. A reporter asked the girl what she thought of the men acting the way they had.

"I really don't understand why they all acted that way. I'm just one girl. All those men are supposed to be the ones in charge of all the money in the country. I mean, I think it must be dangerous or something for all

those men to be only thinking about titty-fucking girls and everything in the middle of the day," said the girl.

The reporters listened to the girl. The reporters crossed out what they had written on their stenographic pads. The reporters frowned. The reporters were silent. The reporters shook their heads.

A reporter asked the girl what her mother thought of what had been happening.

"Oh, she thinks it's just wonderful. She thinks it'll help me catch a husband. Every day she makes herself sick worrying I'm not going to find a man. She says with my picture in the paper the way it was I'll have such a great demand," said the girl.

The reporters listened to the girl. The reporters finished writing on their stenographic pads. The reporters smiled. The reporters laughed. The reporters nodded.

THE PORNOGRAPHER

You recognized me, didn't you? They said in Paris I am the supreme pornographic publisher of Paris. Perhaps you didn't recognize me. These days in the United States I walk down the street and no one knows my face. In Paris I was in the newspapers whenever I was arrested all the time. People cringe sometimes in the street and whisper to each other there is the man who makes the dirty books. The American tourists walked up to me to find where they can buy under the counter all the hot stuff. They drool and shake my hand so I think they are going to attack me.

I can say that I have even had a very large picture in *Le Figaro*. This is a very conservative newspaper. Even their pictures of de Gaulle usually are small. Most of the pornography today is very bad. Very shallow. People very soon will tire of the vulgar erotic sex fiction that is published in the last few years by other publishers. A completely new form of erotic literature will emerge from the dungheap of pornography as it exists today. Today we move to a new, more refined, more complicated category of fiction that is more autobiographical and tolerates a greater erotic content. I know this. This is why I will become one of the greatest successes ever in publishing.

After the sexual revolution we will experience a mystical revolution. From the hippie-yippie development and drugs and the fusion of the oriental disciplines of Yoga and Zen and oriental eroticism will come the basis of tomorrow's style and research. As in everything today this field becomes much more difficult and mysterious so it is impossible for anyone to become a master unless he is a specialist as I am.

After I became famous for publishing Henry Miller and "Marguerite," which no one will touch now, everyone jumps into publishing pornography for dollars. Everywhere competition springs up which seeks to look exactly like myself. My image has been fragmented and appropriated by so many different publishers that I am not myself any longer—and this is a great relief. I became tired of my ancient existence although it was a very great one. Now I can grow into really big business.

I love a lot to work in New York now. I will make a million dollars in six months. There is the competition but I will leave it all far behind. It is wonderful to indulge in business in New York. It is very good to swindle here where everyone swindles everyone else. I have worked for six months to build up my list of titles and to find writers. It seems there is no end to demand for pornography. I have published fifteen books here already. I have more than seventy books and will choose the best to publish. I am bringing my Apollo Press from Paris and also Bedside Books and Olivia Press and will begin other imprints. For instance, some of the ordinary books are "Warm Bodies" and "An Ocean of Flesh" and "Fingers" and "Brothers and Sisters." I choose most of the words for titles myself because I am an expert in titles.

Some people knocked one day at the door of my office in Gramercy Park and said they were members of Parents for Decency or something and they want to inspect my business. So I smile and invite them in and act like a shoe salesman. I ask them what is it you would like to see of my pornography, flagellism if this is your taste, or a book about sucking or sadism, whatever you prefer, perhaps your favorite is intercourse in the anus. They all go out very mad. Pornography is like all business, in which the buyer likes to be cheated but does not want you to tell him you are doing it. If they change the laws of obscenity here after twenty years perhaps I will go into the furniture business and sell false antiques.

Of course some of the pornography publishers in California are completely ridiculous. Their style of provocation is absurd. They make badly illustrated nudic magazines and picture pornography that is supposed to show the different positions of normal fucking and producing excitement and things like this. My books are better, more inventive, more literate. These people, I recognize they must earn a living but really I feel a professional shame and embarrassment for them.

I am invigorated to work in New York. In Paris the police are always cracking down. They say that the police drove me into bankruptcy. This is a lie because I have never been bankrupt. These are rumors started by my enemies who try to embarrass me. I always keep a certain money for capital to begin with something else. It is true they make me serve in the army six months and send me to jail because I publish pornography. Actually this is because of plots of competitors and because I am Jewish. How can you do business with French peasants who take ten years to understand the simplest thing and for whom the word tradition is everything? In New York people realize that life is short. Here business is a game. In France it is a tedious duty to your family and your country.

Once there was a writer who submitted a work of pornography genius to me. I rush to visit his house and find out about this great talent. He lives in the rue de Babylone and I discover that he is a boy of ten who says he uses his imagination. He swears to me he is positive he has had no experience with girls—or boys or whoever—and he writes like a master. Then he starts fucking and pfut he can write nothing. I could have become an actor. They tell me still I look exactly like an actor. With a little difference in luck I could have been lost to the profession of pornography.

My wife asks me what she is to tell my daughter when she asks how I earn our living and I say tell her I am a champion dirty old man. Everyone says pornography is an easy business but this is a lie. I have very quickly earned big fortunes and lost them too. It is very difficult and you have to be very good. In Paris a competitor had me arrested by printing very outrageous pornography over my imprint. Then I print a very deadly and dirty cartoon of de Gaulle over his imprint and he is arrested for treason.

New York is not good for writing erotic literature. The most efficient erotic writers are writers on the West Coast. I fly to the West Coast and back twenty times. There are no masterpieces yet like I have published but it is never masterpieces that earn money. New York is the very best market for erotic writing because of the intensity and nervosity and loneliness. Some authors want me to publish books under their real name. I don't know why but if they ask me I will do this for them. Others have silly pseudonyms like Judd Butte and Daktor del Roccia. These days Western pornography is very popular, with Indians and hunters in the forest who are homosexual. I have several books to exploit this taste which will develop a little and then die. Daktor del Roccia is an American who lives in Paris. He always talks with the third person, never "I," and wears five sweaters at once. He is very strange but has great talent and can write an average book in two weeks and a half.

Some people have slandered me all over the world by saying that I cheat my writers by paying them fifty dollars and taking all of the royalties. This is a lie. I swear this. I give most of my writers two thousand dollars in advance against the royalties. I don't deny that this leaves me enough to become a millionaire. Let's face it, I am in a business, not in the Red Cross. It's me who takes all the risks with the police and must abuse my eyes to read all the laws in the night with my lawyers.

I get hundreds of letters from readers in America of my books. It makes me tired. My correspondence is more aggressive here than in France. People always want you to do something for them. To advise them, to go to bed with them, to confess them. They want a dialogue all the time. There are others who send you letters in which they accumulate all possible obscenities and provocations. If you show the least sympathy for those you're lost, you're swallowed. I have problems enough with my writers who are crazy who need attention.

I have made a deal with Grove Press to distribute my hardcover books. They have tried to take advantage of me but I watch them very carefully. My other books I place with ten wholesalers who are very efficient. The market for books in America is gigantic because everybody buys paperback books in the drugstores. In France I contributed to the propaganda to make more people read books but I think it was hopeless.

I have a pile of manuscripts which increases at my office. It is work to read those. It is true I am a connoisseur of pornography. People believe that I have read everything and can read it quickly and easily and am not affected and this is a great joke but this is not true. If it is bad pornography writing without taste I am indifferent. Then I read something that is good and I become excited. I believe having this sense for telling good from bad is what makes my success. One must be born with this. I believed that reading was to take the place of action. I believed people to be insulted by pornography because this is to admit to the impossibility for them of dramatic action. Now I do not believe this. There is something very mysterious. It has something to do with conception and eroticism. There is something which makes it sometimes more exciting to read than to act. In writing there is appeal to the idea. The idea is the key impulse of eroticism. I become so excited I have to relieve myself. They call these books fuck books but really they are masturbation books. You see a man preferring the idea in the work of Dante.

You see I work too hard in masturbation because I enjoy my work too much. I wish it were possible I did not enjoy my work. It takes too much energy. It is very, very unhealthy for me. I ate too much sweets to keep my energy. From this I suffer from diabetes. From this I suffer from neuropathy of the eyes. Shit, I could go blind. So you see from this that you have absolute proof from me that the fact is true that from jerking you can go blind.

EIGHT

VIOLET AND DAISY

Violet and Daisy died of the flu. Violet and Daisy were sixty years old. Police found Violet and Daisy lying dead on the floor. Violet and Daisy had not reported for work for several days. Violet and Daisy had worked at a supermarket in Charlotte, North Carolina. Violet and Daisy had worked at two weighing counters in a supermarket. Violet and Daisy had come to Charlotte, North Carolina, from Florida in 1960. Violet and Daisy had operated a fruit stand in Florida.

Violet and Daisy were twins. Violet and Daisy were Siamese twins. Violet and Daisy were joined at the base of the spine. Violet and Daisy had attended church. Violet and Daisy had attended the Purcell Methodist Church. Violet and Daisy had no survivors. Violet and Daisy had performed in vaudeville. Violet and Daisy had been a famous vaudeville act.

Violet and Daisy had been born in England. Violet and Daisy's mother had died soon after their birth. Violet and Daisy's father had been killed in the First World War. Violet and Daisy had been taken on a tour of Germany at the age of four. Violet and Daisy had been exhibited in circuses and street carnivals in Austria for three years. Violet and Daisy had come to the United States in 1916.

Violet and Daisy were four feet eleven inches tall. Violet and Daisy together weighed one hundred and ninety pounds, Violet and Daisy were not identical twins. Violet was a brunette. Daisy was a blonde. "We are our own jazz band," Violet and Daisy had said. "We have been studying music via the saxophone," Violet and Daisy had said, "It's lots of fun making a sax do stunts," Violet and Daisy had said. "Especially when there are two of us, with two," Violet and Daisy had said. "So that one can supply what the other misses."

"Houdini taught us to get rid of each other mentally." Violet and Daisy had said. "When Daisy has a date sometimes, I quit paying attention," Violet had said. "Sometimes I read a book," Violet had said, "And sometimes I just take a nap," Violet had said. "Character will accomplish anything for you," Harry Houdini had said. "You must learn to forget your physical link," Harry Houdini had said. "And develop mental independence," Harry Houdini had said. "And you'll get anything you want," Harry Houdini had said.

Violet and Daisy were denied marriage licenses in twenty states. Violet was married to a dancer in 1956. The marriage was annulled. Daisy was married in 1941. Violet and Daisy were twins. Violet and Daisy were Siamese twins. Violet and Daisy died of the flu. Police found Violet and Daisy lying dead on the floor.

WHITE SAND

There was a girl sitting on the side of the hill. There was a boy sitting on the side of the hill. There was a hill. There was the silhouette of the boy and girl sitting on the side of the hill. There were stars in the sky. The hill was gray. There were mountains. There were brown mountains. There were violet mountains. There was a valley.

"We have not been at the kitchen of the Ambassador Hotel," said a man.

"We're not concerned with the assassination of Senator Kennedy specifically," said a man.

"Turn and grab him as if you really wanted him," said the man,

"Oh, Leonardo," said the girl.

"Oh, you Italian pervert," said the girl.

"Do it naturally," said the man.

"Do it in your own manner," said the man.

"It's a borate hill," said a man.

"Excellent," said the man.

"Now we get somewhere," said the man.

"Wherever he goes, symbols crop up," said a man.

"Everywhere, everywhere, symbols," said a man.

"There's a scorpion in a Silex in the Furnace Creek Lodge," said a man.

"It looks like a pet shrimp," said a man.

"He's fifty-six years old," said a man.

"The Black Mountains, the Panamint Mountains," said a man.

There was sand. The sand was gray. There was a gully. A man stood beside the gully. There were footprints in the gray sand.

"He's so seemingly young and so superbly creative," said a man.

"He looks austere," said a man.

"He brought five tons of dry color," said a man.

"He looks like a Renaissance cardinal," said a man.

"You mix it with water," said a man.

"It's enough to spray most of southern California," said a man.

"He painted the grass, trees, buildings in London to get the right texture for 'Focus,' " said a man.

"It looks like the moon," said a man.

"It looks like mounds of congealed oatmeal," said a man.

"Leftovers of a prehistoric breakfast," said a man.

"He probably won't use it," said a man.

"The National Park people would object," said a man.

"He likes it the way it is," said a man.

"Don't lie," said the girl.

"You must never lie to me," said the girl.

"I'm not lying," said the boy.

"You want to," said the girl.

"Yes," said the boy.

"I want you," said the girl.

"Yes," said the boy.

"We must be frank," said the girl.

"Yes," said the boy.

"I'll kill Nicolo," said the boy.

"No, please," said the girl.

"I will," said the boy."

"You love Nicolo," said the boy.

"No," said the girl.

"Nicolo has slept with you," said the boy.

"Yes," said the girl.

"A little plane crashed in the Funeral Mountains last week," said a man.

"It could have been the beginning of one of his scripts," said a man.

"Like the TFX in Nevada," said a man.

"That plane has a fatal flaw," said a man.

"We wanted to do something about contemporary American youth and the political scene," said a man.

"They're on the east on the edge of the valley," said a man.

"It's ambiguous," said a man.

"Uttonnelli is always ambiguous," said a man.

"It concerns an act of political commitment," said a man.

"They found the pilot alive," said a man.

"His passenger became delirious and wandered off," said a man.

"The white-hot sun," said a man.

"Politics is a magnificent theme in his hands," said a man.

"He was wearing only Bermuda shorts," said a man.

"Society moves to crush this pair but they won't be crushed," said the man.

"There are relations between freedom and responsibility," said the man.

"How can one not dedicate his life to creation?" said the man.

"They didn't find him after twenty-four hours," said a man.

"Don't lie," said the girl.

"You must never lie to me," said the girl.

"I'm not lying," said the boy.

"You want me," said the girl.

"Yes," said the boy.

"I want you," said the girl.

"Yes," said the boy.

"I'll kill Nicolo," said the boy.

"No, please," said the girl.

"I will," said the boy.

"You love Nicolo," said the boy.

"No," said the girl.

"Nicolo has made love to you," said the boy.

"Yes," said the girl.

"Zablecki Rock," said a man.

"Speak up," said the man.

"He's making it in the Italian way," said a man.

"Up," said the man.

"Excellent," said the man.

"Now we get somewhere," said the man.

"There are no camera directions," said a man.

There were screeching sounds. There were booming sounds. Airplanes flew over the sand. The girl stroked her hair. The girl's hair was brown.

"It's hardly more than a dialogue treatment," said a man.

"It's all in his head," said a man.

"He fights very hard to remain uncompromised," said a man.

"He doesn't want to be compromised," said a man.

"He wants to stay uncompromised by the mechanics of his craft," said a man.

"There's sand stuck in my bottom," said the girl.

"Call Colonel Trumbull," said a man.

"Get the F-105's out of the north of the valley," said a man.

"She's Doria Hendys," said a man.

"She's nineteen," said a man.

"He's Peter Farkis," said a man.

"He's twenty," said a man.

"They're making their debuts," said a man.

"It is or it isn't about a political assassination," said a man.

"If they knew what we were doing," said a man.

"In the airplanes," said a man.

"They would bomb us," said a man.

"Las Vegas Gunnery Range," said a man.

"Her mother is Anne Hendys," said a man.

"Her mother is director of the Passadena Dance Workshop," said a man.

"It is something like the setting for 'L'Appassionata,' " said the man.

"Except the scale is completely different," said the man.

"I don't care," said the girl.

"I can't wait," said the girl.

"I have to now," said the girl.

"I don't care," said the girl,

"The title is 'Zablecki Rock,' " said a man.

"Take a leak," said the girl.

"Zablecki Rock is down the road," said a man.

"It's a local rock formation," said a man.

"Squat and piss in the sand," said the girl.

"I don't care," said the girl.

"I can piss standing up," said the girl.

"We're going to bus in teenagers," said a man.

"For a love-in," said a man,

"Four hundred teenagers from Salt Lake City and Las Vegas," said a man.

"It'll be rather splendid," said a man.

"Sirhan became committed to his own destruction," said the man.

"What does this say to us about reality?" said the man.

"Everyone can have beauty of spirit," said the man.

"God is dead perhaps," said the man,

"God exists as the principle of the artist," said the man.

"He can fuck me really, I don't care," said the girl.

"Maybe that's what he should do," said the girl.

"There's a postcard showing it," said a man.

"It says it was named after a Mr. Zablecki," said a man.

"Show everything, the hair, I don't care," said the girl.

"You've shown hair before," said the girl.

"I don't care," said the girl.

"Everyone's very, very dedicated," said a man.

"I'm not embarrassed at all," said the girl.

"Why should anyone be embarrassed?" said the girl.

"I'm never embarrassed about anything, only hypocrites are," said the girl.

"You want me," said the girl.

"Yes," said the boy.

"I want you," said the girl.

"Yes," said the boy.

"We must be frank," said the girl.

The sun rose. The violet mountains became blue. The hill became white. There was white sand. There were trucks. Trucks moved on the white sand.

"I don't care, I'll do anything," said the girl.

"There'll be a love-in on a gypsum-borate plateau," said a man.

"George Hardy and twenty members of his Pop Theater troupe will come," said a man.

"A scorcher," said a man.

"I'm not a virgin, you know," said the girl.

"I take pills, I took my pill," said the girl.

"He's not even excited, I'm excited," said the girl.

"They always want to close the set," said the girl.

"Girls have vulvas, boys have penises, so what?" said the girl.

"I was associate producer of 'Gretel, Gretel,' " said a man.

"It's the first thing I've produced," said a man.

"It's the first time he's worked in the U.S.," said a man.

"We're telling it as it is," said the girl.

"Why not?" said the girl.

"For three mill we should have a portable john," said a man.

"This light is fantastic," said the man.

"His adaptability is marvelous," said a man.

"Damn," said a man.

"There isn't much he isn't showing," said a man.

"And he'll get away with it," said a man.

"We won't get an X," said a man.

"We'll get an XX," said a man.

"It's going to show the truth, it really is," said the girl.

"Look at his nose," said the girl.

"His nose is so straight," said the girl.

"It's like a ruler," said the girl.

"He's so handsome," said the girl.

"Mr. Zablecki was an early executive of the Borax Company," said a man.

"No one knows Mr. Zablecki's first name," said a man.

"Mr. Zablecki's first name seems to have been forgotten," said a man.

"Well," said the girl.

"I certainly don't feel I'm being molded," said the girl.

"If that's what you mean," said the girl.

"I feel I'm doing my own thing," said the girl.

"You have such nice sideburns," said the girl.

"My jacket is skunk, real skunk," said the girl.

"It is about freedom," said the man.

"What is there, really, besides the truth?" said the girl.

"He's the only one that wants to tell the truth," said the girl.

"I don't know what God has to do with anything," said the girl.

"I know what I want," said the girl.

"I recognize it's a tremendous opportunity for me," said the boy.

"It's Nehi or Dr. Pepper," said a man.

"It's a political story but it's also a love story," said a man.

"It's a rattlesnake skin," said the girl.

"I'm going to roll it up and make a necklace out of it," said the girl.

"Motta skinned it," said the girl.

"This is really going to grab people," said a man.

"I hope there aren't many snakes," said the boy.

"Everyone wants to break through the phoniness of our culture," said the boy.

"It more or less does away with the phony romance surrounding sex," said the boy.

"It's an unearthly landscape," said a man.

"The boy and girl are trying to discover themselves," said the girl.

"There's a little pimple there," said the girl. "I don't care, it's the truth, young people have pimples, that's all," said the girl.

"My mother wasn't quite sure she wanted me to or not," said the girl.

"I've always known what I want," said the girl.

"I suppose I like my mother, I respect her," said the girl.

"The present leaders of society have failed and they know it," said the girl.

"I went into the Desert Inn," said the boy,

"I hated school, I'd never go to college," said the girl.

"They exploit bare breasts but I don't think what they do is really very sexy," said the boy.

"Uttonnelli discourages the usual production publicity," said a man.

"He does not need publicity to give him an identity," said a man.

"He fired two unit publicity agents in the first two months," said a man.

"A girl wanted me to lay her in the Desert Inn," said the boy.

"A girl came up to me in the Desert Inn," said the boy,

"I think women's breasts aren't very good looking if the nipples are too large," said the boy,

"He's doing a just fabulous job," said a man.

"It's a sheephearder's hat," said the girl.

"L.A. is all right, it's getting creative now," said the boy.

"I wonder what it would be like to make love in orbit," said the boy.

"It's the first time anyone's tried to show young people like us in America the way they are," said the girl,

"They say I look like David Hemmings," said the boy.

"I want to be myself," said the boy.

"I won't be drafted, I was born at sea," said the boy.

"Hot wind," said a man.

"It has to be controversial," said a man.

"The country is going to get it whether it's controversial or not," said a man.

"My head bursts with ideas," said the man.

"There is so much here in America for art," said the man.

"They use so little," said the man.

"The religion of artists must be novelty," said the man.

"We want to show how people can interract without destroying the other person's freedom," said the girl.

"The mother doesn't understand anything," said the girl.

"There's absolutely no way to get a start," said the boy.

"TV offers nothing," said the boy.

"I've never even gone to New York," said the boy.

"She's fabulous to work with," said the boy.

"I suppose I'll marry some actress or someone pretty soon," said the boy.

"I'm not getting much for this," said the girl.

"I don't care," said the girl.

"People don't realize that for all of us love is everything," said the girl.

"War just goes on," said the girl.

"They send men off to fight and never ask them what they want," said the girl.

"You can't let yourself get dragged into anything you don't believe in," said the girl.

"I don't think it makes any difference how a person earns their living," said the girl.

"You can't let noncreative work interfere with your awareness of what's important," said the girl.

"Girls aren't going to let society treat them that way," said the girl.

"Girls aren't going to be just housewives," said the girl.

"If you have enough to live on," said the girl.

"What else do you need?" said the girl.

"I'm positive of this," said the girl.

"I've read 'Chamade,' " said the girl.

"She's my favorite writer," said the girl.

"I've read a lot of existential novels," said the girl.

"I'm an existentialist," said the girl.

The boy and the girl smoked cigarettes. Smoke came out of the noses of the boy and the girl. Smoke drifted across the sand.

"Communication," said the girl.

"To show how people can cooperate instead of competing all the time," said the girl.

"My pack of Slims is at the Lodge," said the girl.

"There's nobody that can match this man," said a man.

"To me he's way above Fellini," said a man.

"It's so stupid," said the girl.

"It's silly," said the girl.

"We just won't stand for any hypocracy," said the girl.

"Not in any part of our lives," said the girl.

"All of us feel this way," said the girl.

"If a girl and boy could just stay out here in a cabin," said the girl.

"Just to be alone with your lover," said the girl.

"My mother doesn't mind what I do," said the girl.

"I want to go to Italy," said the girl.

"Italian films have always been my favorite," said the girl.

"She's only getting ten thou," said a man.

"I really worship him," said the girl.

"I feel I'm an instrument of something," said the girl.

"I'd do anything he asked me to," said the girl.

"Because Uttonnelli is the greatest genius," said the girl.

"I'm so happy," said the girl.

"I know this is going to be a classic," said the girl.

"It's hard to walk on sand," said the boy.

"I hate walking on sand," said the boy.

"It's Nixon," said a man.

"It's not ideological as far as I know," said a man.

"Humphrey, Nixon," said a man.

"I think democracy is dying," said the boy.

"I wouldn't vote," said the boy.

"Even if they lowered the age," said the boy.

"Miami and Chicago showed the parties don't have any respect for young people," said the girl.

"Some of these people voted this morning," said a man,

"There has to be a completely new kind of politics," said the girl.

"I think we'll start a trend," said the girl.

"I can't watch most movies," said the boy.

"They're so completely false," said the boy.

"Politics just makes you sick," said the boy.

There were boxes on the white sand. There was a mirror. The girl looked in the mirror. The girl stroked her hair.

"I see the script, I see everything immediately," said the man.

"No one can solve problems today," said the man.

"No one sees these problems as they are," said the man.

"In art it is possible to see these problems," said the man.

"Ordinary people just don't try," said the girl.

"Most people are already dead," said the girl.

"We want to show a certain personal relationship," said the girl.

"Most people just don't do what they really want to do," said the girl.

"McCarthy puzzles me," said a man.

"I hated restaurant work," said the girl.

"Excellent," said the man.

"Now we get somewhere," said the man,

"I laid her one time in Santa Monica," said a man.

"She won't admit it," said a man.

"She'd kill me for saying it," said a man.

"I have the feeling this is going to bomb," said a man.

"Does she suck?" said a man.

"I didn't ask her," said a man.

"We'll go to Los Angeles," said the boy.

"I don't know," said the girl.

"We must go," said the boy.

"I don't know," said the girl.

"You're so anxious," said the girl.

"I want you to stay with me," said the boy.

"Yes," said the girl.

"You don't respect me," said the boy.

"Yes, I do," said the girl.

"You'll betray me," ssid the boy.

"No," said the girl.

"I'm afraid," said the boy.

"What will happen?" said the boy.

"What will we do?" said the boy.

"Trust me, please," said the girl.

"Can I?" said the boy.

"Yes," said the girl.

"You have to believe in what you're doing," said the girl.

"You can't be committed to only yourself," said the girl.

"There should be a political party just for people who think like young people," said the girl,

"I'd like to fuck her," said a man.

"You'd like to fuck everything," said a man.

"Don't discourage me," said a man.

"It's just impossible for a lot of conventional people to know what's happening now," said the girl.

"It's so disgusting," said the girl.

"People marry and rot," said the girl.

"Her mouth is too big to be a star," said a man.

"He always uses girls with big mouths," said a man.

"I'd never act in any play," said the girl.

"Doing plays is obsolete," said the girl.

"He's got a good lawyer," said a man.

"Spreading his income over five years," said a man.

"I'm short," said a man.

"Litton Industries stock," said a man.

"She worked in the Beverly Hilton Restaurant," said a man.

"She's Hecksler's girl all right," said a man.

"If Farkis knew," said a man.

"It's a cactus flower," said the girl.

"What kind of cactus flower is that?" said the girl.

"It's such a beautiful little thing," said the girl.

"It's Farkis and her every night they get a chance," said a man.

"This pair are good because they play who?" said the man.

"Themselves, they are authentic," said the man.

"The result of crime is always more crime," said the man.

"Love is always the solution," said the man.

"I must be very deliberate," said the man.

"This will be the consummation of everything," said the man.

"Hecksler introduced her to the producers and Uttonnelli," said a man.

"Hecksler would kill her," said a man.

"Hecksler thinks it's a secret," said a man.

"He always wants her at his place Sunday afternoons," said a man.

"There should be communities," said the girl.

"You have to think," said the girl.

"You have to decide what you want to do," said the girl.

"I don't understand," said the girl.

"How can they put a person in prison for possessing marijuana?" said the girl.

"If a person likes to use drugs," said the girl.

"I took methamphetamine twice and it didn't hurt me at all," said the girl.

"Excellent," said the man.

"Now we get somewhere," said the man.

"I am very surprised and pleased with the rangers," said a man.

"We've received fine cooperation," said a man.

"I mean we look like a bunch of lunatics," said a man.

"I'm not sure I agree with capitalism," said the girl.

"I mean Uttonnelli and the rest of us aren't exactly in their lifestyle," said a man.

"There was a Marcia Gelson," said a man.

"He gave her Marcia's part," said a man.

"Marcia was a better actress," said a man.

"I guess Hecksler's still married," said a man.

"Hecksler's coming here," said a man.

"If Farkis starts talking about himself and her," said a man.

"Hecksler must be sixty," said a man.

"Her mother knows Hecksler," said a man.

"You are leaving there and walking there to talk some more," said the man.

"Don't gasp," said the man.

"Act like you control your voice with difficulty," said the man.

"You must touch each other with passion," said the man.

"Good, you have lust," said the man.

"Excellent," said the man.

"Now we get somewhere," said the man.

"This must be perfect," said the man.

"Sand gets in my scalp," said a man.

"We go up to there and stop?" said the boy.

"Yes," said the man.

"How do you pick us up?" said the boy.

"We dub," said the man.

"In Italy we dub everything," said the man.

"We're showing masturbation, everything," said the girl.

"When you think of what they do to Negroes," said the girl.

"People should be fair and considerate," said the girl.

"Because life is just dull," said the girl.

"If you're not a genius like he is or something," said the girl.

"If everyone could just live together quietly and control the population," said the girl.

"I play basketball," said the boy.

"Her father works for the Bank of America," said a man.

"Well, we don't have to worry about rain," said a man.

"He has a certain very definite vision," said a man.

"The youngsters will save us," said the man.

"Sometimes I feel a despair about the world," said the man.

"This is very seldom," said the man.

"It is art but it is work," said the man.

"Bergman I do not prefer," said the man.

"He is the style-setter," said a man.

"This is the first time he's ever worked in the US," said a man.

"If this doesn't click it's salve Italia for him," said a man.

"She turned over Hurd," said a man.

"Hurd tried suicide twice," said a man.

"Nin had an abortion in Colorado," said a man.

"Some people just can't take it," said a man.

"She and Hecksler are going to Europe," said a man.

"Hecksler owns bean fields," said a man.

"There's a restaurant on Forty-Ninth Street, the Golden Horn," said a man.

"Who swiped the ice?" said a man.

"Talk about takes," said a man.

"Fifteen takes," said a man.

"I think I can say this is going to be a masterpiece," said a man.

"At ten-thirty we go to the highway," said the man.

"We will go to Bad Water this afternoon," said the man.

"We will get impressions of the Natural Bridge," said the man.

"Sunset Boulevard is a fine place, very desolate," said the man.

"I love that bandana," said the man.

"Everyone seeks happiness, but how is this possible today?" said the man.

"The love story, this is the basis for everything," said the man.

"Violence, injustice, inhumanity of today, all this must be included," said the man,

"I aim at art, not teaching, but if I teach, all right too," said the man.

"We'll go to Los Angeles," said the boy.

"I don't know," said the girl.

"We must go," said the boy.

"I don't know," said the girl,

"You're so anxious," said the girl,

"I want you to stay with me," said the boy.

"Yes," said the girl.

"You don't respect me," said the boy.

"Yes, I do," said the girl.

"You'll betray me," said the boy.

"No," said the girl.

"I'm afraid," said the boy.

"What will happen?" said the boy.

"What will we do?" said the boy.

"Trust me, please," said the girl.

"Can I?" said the boy.

"Yes," said the girl.

"Excellent," said the man.

"Now we get somewhere," said the man,

"The pair are not rebelling," said the man.

"They pay absolutely no attention to the rules of society," said the man.

"Today I'm about ready to retire to the Country Home," said a man.

"What a racket," said a man.

"Next he'll probably make something about homosexual astronauts," said a man.

"Well, where's the twenty-mule team?" said a man.

"I know girls will identify with me," said the girl,

"You have to be more than a pretty face," said the girl.

"Technically it's a Hollywood job," said a man.

"It'll cost three million," said a man.

"He's making it around Los Angeles, Arizona and here," said a man.

"Carlo Ponti for Metro," said a man.

"Just so nobody gets killed with an axe," said a man.

"We're under budget so far," said a man.

"She can always go back to the Hilton," said a man.

"Hecksler gives her an allowance," said a man.

"She really likes Hecksler," said a man.

"Hecksler slugged Renee," said a man.

"When she left him," said a man.

"They'll be fighting like dogs," said a man.

"Hecksler and his girls always end up fighting like dogs," said a man.

"If people would just let people alone," said the girl.

"People have to take care of each other," said the girl.

"What they teach you is all wrong," said the girl.

"Hollywood seethes with rumors about our work," said a man.

"Controversial subject matter," said a man.

"I wouldn't go near Hecksler," said a man.

"Hecksler's poison," said a man.

"Why would anybody want to become a movie star?" said a man.

"Watch it," said a man.

"The sun will give you cancer," said a man.

"So Novarro got it," said a man.

"Pretty shabby," said a man.

"A friend of his—some friend," said a man.

"It's her life," said a man.

"It's her problem," said a man.

"She's lucky she's got this far," said a man.

"She should marry a real estate agent," said a man.

"Poor Susie Franchette, she wanted too much," said a man.

"Any girl looks good with her legs in the air," said a man.

The boy and the girl stood on the white sand. The boy and the girl walked on the white sand. There was a bird. There was a white cliff.

"He looks like my brother," said the girl.

"I used to kiss my brother in the bathtub," said the girl.

"I know Hecksler," said a man.

"It won't last," said a man.

"It never lasts," said a man.

"Yes," said a man.

"Who has the candy?" said a man.

"But does she know that?" said a man.

NINE

THE ACTRESS

She died in an Antibes clinic. She was born in London. She lived in a villa she bought with her share of the proceeds of "The Congress Dances." She was sixty-one years old. She acted in an average of four motion pictures a year. She was married three times. When she fell in love with Willy Fritsch their romance was celebrated throughout the world. She spoke thirteen languages. She acted in motion pictures in four languages. She made her debut as a dancer in Berlin after World War I. Richard Eichberg gave her roles in "The Crowd Entertains Itself" and "The Road from Paradise." At the outbreak of World War II she fled to the United States. She acted in the theater for a while. Her fame soon diminished. She was never able to reestablish herself in motion pictures. She acted in "Suzanne the Chaste," "Miquette and Her Mother," "Serenade" and "Blonde Dream." At the height of her career a Hungarian nobleman offered her a castle and an entire village to go with it. In Antibes she operated a souvenir shop and raised edible snails. Her hair was blonde. Her hair was beautiful. The castle is now a tractor factory.

SCENE

She sniffled. She coughed. She sniffled. "Dreading," she said,

"Dreading seeing it," she said,

"I really dread to see it," she said.

"Just," she said.

"Dread," she said.

"It's rather funny," she said. "I wore sheets," she said,

"Because we pretended to be angels," she said.

"When I was five," she said.

"We dressed out the Yorkshire terrier as the devil," she said.

"Cousins and me," she said.

"In the least," he said.

"I'm not embarrassed," he said.

"She would never do anything," he said.

"In the least," he said.

"Childhood in Scotland," she said.

"To embarrass me," he said.

"They use words like 'shit' and 'bitch' and 'bugger,' " she said.

She coughed. She sniffled. She wiped her eyes. There was a hotel. She sighed. She shrugged. She sniffled. She coughed. She coughed. There was blue light.

"Broad-minded," he said.

"I'm broad-minded," he said.

"Rather broad-minded," he said.

"Broad-minded, you know," he said.

"You know," he said.

"To make it more realistic," she said.

"The ugly stepsister," she said.

"A family production," she said.

"Cinderella," she said.

"I played in my dramatic debut," she said.

"It makes for a maturer attitude," she said.

"You know," she said.

"It makes it more honest," she said.

"You know," she said.

"A lot of people use language like that," she said.

"I suppose I have the sort of mind that takes the over-all view," she said.

"It's good," she said.

"Good if it's not, well," she said.

"Overdone," she said.

"You know," she said.

"Overdone," she said.

"I suppose it often gets me into trouble, perhaps," she said.

"Not one frame of it," she said.

"He hasn't seen a frame of the scene," she said.

"Modern," she said.

"For instance," she said.

"If you want to be specific," she said.

"Specific," she said.

"Talk about the scene," she said.

"Specific," she said.

"Think," she said.

"Let me," she said.

"Think," she said.

"A minute," she said.

"I'll try to get my point of view," she said.

"Modern attitude towards sex," she said.

"He'll see it tonight," she said.

"He's a courageous man," she said.

"People do associate blue eyes and blond hair with angels," she said.

"Willy," she said.

"Willy-nilly," she said.

"I was stunned that people should see me that way," she said.

"They do, don't they?" she said.

"They do," she said.

"They pre-conceive you," she said.

"Just dread," she said.

"Dread," she said.

"Even that," she said.

"Unauthorized *Playboy* magazine layout," she said.

"That didn't budge it," she said.

"One just dreads to be pre-conceived," she said.

"One is always fighting it," she said.

"Enlarge," he said.

"She wanted to enlarge," he said.

"Enlarge," he said.

"You know, expand," he said.

"Sweet young thing," she said.

"Seven years ago," she said.

"I had two film credits," she said.

"An image problem," she said,

"It began simply enough," she said,

"I was a bare twenty," she said.

"The Breck shampoo girl," she said.

"Typecast as a sweet young thing," she said.

"Come to life," she said.

She coughed. She sneezed. She coughed. She shook her head. She put on a gray sweater. There was a sweater.

"Two lines in the script," she said.

"Well," she said.

"Well," she said.

"First of all," she said.

"If we're going to be specific," she said.

"It was just two lines," she said.

"Exposition in the script," she said.

"I'm not so totally humorless," she said,

"Rushing naked into the ocean," she said.

"And I appear today," she said.

"Totally humorless," she said.

"Humorless," she said.

"Surreptitious," she said.

"They don't show today," she said.

"After all," she said.

"Hardly anything," she said.

"While filming 'The Seventh Day,' " she said.

"You're getting me on rather an intense subject," she said.

"Naked," she said.

"Surreptitiously photographed sequence," she said.

"And the crowning insult," she said,

"Betsy is on the bed playing with her dolls," she said.

"She drops them," she said.

"It went," she said.

"Five minute bedding scene," she said.

"To act," she said.

"Acting," she said.

"Explicit," she said.

"During some of it," he said.

"It's possible to go too far," he said.

"I was there," he said.

"She doesn't belong only to me," he said.

"But with taste," he said.

"My wife is an artist," he said.

"The whole thing about acting," she said.

"Why I act," she said.

"I keep coming up with different answers," she said.

"Mrs. Barnes sits on the bed," she said.

"Near Betsy," she said.

"On the bed," she said.

"Bed," she said.

"Explicit scene," she said.

"Even that," she said.

"That didn't stop them," she said.

"Scripts containing parts of soap-ads girls came in and nothing seemed to be able to stop it," she said.

"The photographer actually came to me," she said.

"First you think it might be the glory," she said.

"The fame," she said.

"But it's not that at all," she said.

"At all," she said.

"Not," she said.

"Most explicit of an American film," she said.

She sneezed. She coughed. She sneezed. She smiled. She frowned.

"When you played Puck," she said.

"You think back," she said.

" 'Midsummer Night's Dream,' " she said.

"That magnificent flying sort of ecstasy," she said.

"He would give me the negatives," she said.

"When you are Puck and as light as air," she said.

"And omnipotent," she said.

"Climax," she said.

"And the scene reaches a dramatic climax," she said.

"Something like that," she said.

"Nothing beyond that," she said.

"That was all it was," she said.

"All," she said,

"All," she said.

"I refused," she said.

"Negatives," she said.

"If I would pay him what *Playboy* would," she said.

"Then when," she said.

"They appeared," she said.

"Then when," she said.

"I mean," she said.

"I enjoy sex and all," she said.

"I mean," she said.

"Sex," she said.

"Sex," she said.

"Vulnerable," she said.

"I felt so vulnerable," she said.

"Shattered," she said.

"I was absolutely shattered," she said.

"So," she said.

"Everyone is so liberal today," she said.

"You," she said.

"You think that's it," she said.

"Omnipotent," she said.

"The heady mountaintops," she said.

"But no," she said.

"Of course it's not something exactly you'd really want small children to go to," he said,

"We married in nineteen sixty," she said.

"Dramatic Arts," she said.

"Royal Academy," she said,

"Two years at the Royal Academy of Dramatic Arts," she said.

"I can remember seeing him," she said.

"I saw him," she said.

"That boy's got super hair but it needs cutting," she said.

"Improper," he said.

"We're both professional actors," he said.

"If I thought there was anything improper," he said.

"I'm not embarrassed for her in the least," he said.

"Actors have to do lots of things," he said.

"I thought," she said.

"That's really why I love acting," she said.

"Lots," he said.

"Why it's so fascinating to me," she said.

"The real things in life," she said.

"They are," she said.

"Aren't they?" she said.

"Sweet," she said.

"Isn't he?" she said.

"So," she said,

"Vulnerable," she said.

"Vulnerable," she said.

"There's very little that's more vulnerable," she said.

"I think," she said,

"To be an actor," she said.

"You're a writer," she said.

"He's so sweet," she said.

"It's your book," she said.

"You're a painter," she said.

"It's your painting," she said.

"You're an actor," she said.

"It's you," she said.

"It's you," she said.

"Your face," she said.

"Your skin," she said.

"Your body," she said.

She sneezed. She coughed. She sighed. She blew her nose. There was blue light in the room. There was snow. She embraced a pillow. There was a pillow. There was a fire. She sniffled. She coughed.

"About yourself and about other people," she said.

"Body," she said.

"Face," she said.

"Skin," she said.

"So cold," she said.

"There's so much to discover," she said,

"Snow," she said.

"Hong Kong flu," she said.

"Somebody once," she said.

"The point," she said.

"Somebody once said to me," she said.

"After I left school I acquired an agent," she said.

"The point of the theater," she said.

"The point of why do any of it," she said.

"You hope for that moment," she said.

"The hope," she said.

"People will leave bigger than when they came in," she said.

"But," she said.

"You can have a rather lot of failures," she said.

"On the whole," he said,

"My last role," he said.

"On the whole," he said.

"I played a detective," he said.

"It was rather challenging," he said.

"Well," she said.

"They can have all that," she said,

"They can take your body and your face," she said.

"But," she said.

"Nobody can take your thoughts," she said.

"He was a super actor," she said.

"I heard him do an audition," she said.

"Marvelous voice," she said.

"I thought," she said.

"It was something Bob evolved," she said.

"He was as frightened as any of us," she said.

"I was very frightened," she said.

"And then one day I did cut his hair," she said.

"Before I went to Hollywood," she said.

"Alec Guiness's daughter in 'Black Watch,' " she said.

"Lunch with Bob," she said.

"A scene like that," she said.

"Scene," she said.

"Strong scene," she said.

"He said this will be strong," she said.

"Unless you're drunk," she said.

"You'll have to be prepared," she said.

"You can't do a scene like that," she said.

"I wasn't drunk," she said.

"Without trust," she said.

" 'Yes,' I said," she said.

" 'Right,' I said," she said.

"I worried horribly," she said.

"At least I can't," she said.

"Nothing specific was discussed," she said.

"Over a period of two or three days," she said.

"It was a difficult period," she said.

"You don't stay at the same level of trust," she said.

"In fact," she said.

"Nothing during the first two thirds of shooting was discussed," she said.

"Specific," she said.

"Difficult for me," she said.

"Difficult for her," she said.

"Absolute," he said,

"Difficult for me and difficult for her," she said.

"An English adolescent in 'The End of Innocence,'" she said.

"She's an absolute genius," he said.

"Conveying the honest interpretation," he said.

"Conveying," he said.

"Vulgar," he said.

"So I know," he said.

"Never," he said.

"Won't be vulgar," he said.

"I know it won't be vulgar," he said.

"Violated," she said.

"Never," he said.

"Whatever," she said.

"Whatever your rational mind says," she said.

She stood up. She sat down. She sniffled. She laughed. She coughed.

"You can't help feeling violated," she said.

"Rational mind," she said.

"Whatever," she said.

"One realized," she said.

"I don't know," she said.

"I just felt like a silver birch all alone on the plain with snow," she said.

"It felt like there was an awful lot of air and wind about," she said.

"One realized there was going to be a seduction scene," she said.

"Of course," she said.

"But," she said.

"Of course there are real people like that," she said.

"Of course," she said.

"They do things like that," she said.

"I was in 'Fanny,' " she said.

"Virginal innocent," she said.

"In 'Fanny' I was," she said.

"Virginal innocent," she said.

"We met some people like that filming," she said.

"Was," she said.

"In 'Doctor Freud,' " she said.

"John Gielgud," she said.

"It's like the Arab," she said.

"Arab," she said.

"What terrified me," she said.

"Arab," she said.

"What worried me," she said.

"Dread," she said.

"Just," she said.

"Sucking," she said.

"Sucking on people's breasts," she said.

"He feels someone is taking his soul," she said. "Dread to be photographed," she said.

"Arab," she said.

"Quite deliberately," she said.

"The role of a promiscuous girl in 'Dugan,' " she said.

"The fear that this moment," she said.

"I can't answer," she said.

"Whether I regret it," she said,

"I was not going to be mine any more," she said.

"They'll probably make films much more this way and we'll look back," she said.

"With a sense of balance," she said.

"Sense," she said.

"Sense of," she said.

"To look," she said.

"Bob told me it would take a long, long time for me," she said.

"I read the script," she said.

"Last year," she said.

"Directed by my husband," she said.

"In a film," she said.

"I'd like to be," she said.

"Passive lesbian named Betsy," she said.

"Anyway," she said.

"Then came D-Day," she said.

"He pushes me very hard," she said.

"Not for some time," she said.

"He's got a marvelous sense of humor," she said.

"Obviously I'm biased," she said.

"Know whether what I did was a good or bad thing," she said.

"To put together in a montage," she said.

"Obviously," she said.

"He wanted a lot of film," she said.

"Play out scene," she said.

"Bob sat down and talked with her and me for a long time and he talked about it for a long time," she said.

"From which to catch bits and seconds," she said.

"He wanted the scene played out," she said.

"He told us," she said.

"Personally," she said.

"He explained why he believed he needed the scene," she said.

"Personally, I can't see how two woman could do that," she said.

"No," she said.

"It's not a montage," she said.

"Taken advantage of," she said.

"No," she said.

"I don't think I was," she said.

"I don't think I was quite as embarrassed as I thought I would be," she said.

"Money," she said.

"I should give mine to the Lesbos Society," she said.

"To buy bras," she said.

" 'Panorama' with Warren Beatty," she said.

"I'll start on 'Don't Eat My Pigs,' " she said.

"He's a teddy bear," she said,

"I used to become annoyed," she said.

"The teddy bear hugs became bottom pinches," she said.

"Valid," he said.

"Artistically valid," he said.

"I don't object," he said.

"She's old enough," he said.

"If it's valid," he said.

"Judgment," he said.

"Taste," he said.

"Valid," he said.

"Valid," he said.

"Taste," he said.

"I don't know what money has to do with it," she said.

"I thought," she said.

"I might be giving too much away," she said.

"Splash," she said.

"I know," she said,

"To make a splash," she said.

"I thought," she said.

"I didn't do it," she said.

"I know he didn't," she said.

"I thought that scene might be the thing," she said.

"The sheer fact of being undressed," she said.

"To chip my soul away," she said.

"Of having to expose yourself," she said.

"Money is nice," she said.

"I could have worked in something else," she said.

She sighed. She sniffled. She coughed. She wiped her eyes. She held a handkerchief. There was a window. She coughed. She kissed.

"Horribly difficult to do it," she said.

"Horribly," she said.

"Horribly," she said.

"Kiss him," she said.

"Prove to you," she said.

"Isn't he?" she said.

"Sweet," she said.

"So," she said.

"Really," she said.

"Actually," she said.

"Not," she said.

"Kiss," she said.

"I'm not queer," she said.

"Not," she said.

"Not," she said.

"Not," she said.

TEN

A VERY QUEER THING

It was a real queer thing, you know. They figured all of us were cracked when we told them about it. They showed us pictures. They wanted to see if we could identify him. Charlie dragged his body off, you see. I couldn't really identify him good. Ritchie said he got more of a look at him. They say he was some Marine that was missing from Da Nang since 1965. We were beating the bushes twenty-four clicks from Phu Bai. We pounded around for a while and took a break and broke out some C's. We were sitting around in this cup of rocks. He stepped out from behind this rock. We could see right away he was an American— Caucasian, a white man, you know. He had a regular M-16 in assault position. His clothes were all kind of tattered. We watched him make a hand signal to his deuce point. The deuce point came up. The deuce point was a regular gook. They stood there talking like they were discussing the matter. They'd been following us. We were surprised to see him. We usually don't come across anybody. He looked something like me. Ritchie thought at first it was me going down to the creek to fill up the canteens. We didn't know what the shit was coming off. We held up for a few seconds. He wasn't no prisoner. He was leading these guys. Ritchie sprayed him across the chest. He fell down on the ground. After a while, another of their patrols got around our flank and opened up. We got out of there but after we went a ways they got Feeney through the ear and we carried Feeney's body out. So while he'd been lying on the ground there he said, "Help me, help me," real plain in English, you know. So I helped him out and sprayed him again.

THE SECURITY ADVISOR

"When we came in of course you had the very overheated US-SU counterstance and we had an atmosphere of strain and Moscow had a forward attitude and was very optimistic," he said.

He sat behind his desk in a swivel chair. There were three journalists sitting in the room.

"I think taking the overview and to give a sweeping judgment we see there has been positive growth in a great many facets. Our broad status shows more positive elements now than when we came in. We have blocked out the effective vector along which it will be possible to positively move. We have overturned some very intractable threats and gone up against challenges which we have been able to minimize successfully and we have surpassed in nearly every instance those who set up to hinder us and I think we leave a much stronger establishment and some very healthy prospects. Taken together it has been I think a quite rewarding and successful tenure for us and I am very happy about it.

"Even with Viet Nam and the flareups we have succeeded very well in translating the mutual posture from wide-ranging, across-the-board confrontation into a new posture where we can narrow on certain areas and exhibit common interests and we have each side working in a specific way to move in and define acceptable understandings and this is very hopeful.

"As a consequence of this we find a measurably augmented facility for unencumbered communication and even when we are custodians as the two principal players in the nuclear game this penetrates even though we have a certain screen of misinterpretation and contradiction of design," he said.

"Then you would say that of your accomplishments you consider the greatest one avoiding another world war?" said a journalist.

"Now we have the category of economics here and in the underdevelopeds and I can say here we have built a very strong success factor because if you juxtapose the expansion rates of our eight years with any other you find a continuous positive curve that overshadows them by several magnitudes and if you approximate the Soviet growth-rate indices you get the readout that Soviet rates are flattening while the free system has accelerating indicators in all categories. So there has been rapid decay of the concept of the Soviet as number two but fast closing the gap and destined to be number one within a finite frame.

"The men with their fingers on policy in the East and everywhere are thinking of optimum economic models for techno-industrial societies in terms of not the Soviet Union or China but Japan, Western Europe, Canada, the United States, Australia.

"In fact you see today in the proto-industrial societies for the first time a very large-scale swing from the formulation that was defended by a good many Westerners as well as the communists that in the area of capital utilization, imposition of reasonable measures for discipline and upgrading growth rates the communists management can rate above a free system and we have seen this school utterly disproved," he said.

"I guess the United States rate of growth was five per cent last year," said a journalist.

"About five per cent. We can look around the countries of the West and sample this rapid forward trend with South Korea, Colombia, Mexico, Taiwan, Iran, and you get the very promising result that there are none of the political units which have reason to have a low level of confidence in the compatibility of growth with cultural and traditional national preoccupations. On the other side of the table under communist programs there are only very negative figures, in Cuba, the Chicoms, where they have probably lower production totals in '68 than in '58, North Korea, North Viet Nam," he said.

"What are the things that you've been most concerned with while you've served here?" said a journalist.

"The main points of our policy have moved ahead, quarantining Castro, functioning bilaterally and directly to reinforce the structures experiencing pressure from infiltration from Cuba, applying some quiet preventive medicine here to preclude establishment of mainland bases which is the short-range goal of their map for Latin America.

"We have been building up acceleration behind the Alliance for Progress at higher rates and we have overcome the initial inertia of the span of two or three years but we have a pretty nominal target curve since '65 and the first Punta del Este," he said.

"The Alliance is beginning to bear fruit then," said a journalist.

"There are certain unresolved anomalies, Castro, a high-danger force, an annoying factor, but certainly very containable but the critical evidence is that you have absolutely no operative force in Latin America which is approaching problems with reference to the Cuban program," he said.

"What was the single most critical period you've experienced," said a journalist.

"We have established crucial guidelines of procedure that set a precedent in response to the brinkmanship strategy, a counter to the Khrushchev gambit of blackmail, of pressure on Berlin in '61 and '62 when he calculated that against the move of a threat of general nuclear attack and pressure against a point of maximum vulnerability we would choose the road of significant diplomatic concessions but Kennedy called the bluff. So you have the example of Berlin and the Cuban missile business which radically reduces the possibility of their choosing the option of pressing diplomacy against the backdrop of nuclear exchange to manageable magnitude.

"With Europe and NATO there was the difficulty of the French, the French position on integration and abandonment of the concept of coordination of the forces in a strategy.

"President Johnson recognized the correct course of movement to cooperation where there was any opening and conscientious reluctance to pursue paths possibly conducing to more coolness," he said.

"What was President Johnson's personal opinion of de Gaulle?" said a journalist.

"You have unexampled achievement in the meeting this April in Washington in tribute to the NATO twentieth anniversary where there is a defensive alliance of twenty years of nations surviving twenty years of peace and committing their safety to carrying it into the future as the essential tool for insuring security. Does this microphone take us all in without moving it?" he said.

"You can be twenty feet away. It's a very good machine," said a journalist.

"How much do you want?" he said.

"My boss said about thirty-five hundred," said a journalist.

"Somebody said the cassette runs for an hour without having to turn it over," said a journalist.

"Where are the photographers for you guys?" he said.

"Well, as to me, Bob didn't want any new photography. He might run a stock shot of you," said a journalist.

"Do you want to say anything more about NATO?" said a journalist.

"We have experienced a decided shift of perspective from the aspect of military to cooperation in the political area looking to the direction of deescalation in Middle Europe and exploring avenues of upgrading contacts between the alliance and the Warsaw group. I think we can look forward to some profound developments along these lines, manpower pull-back, more sweeping East-West understandings of course provided the Kremlin and the Eastern governments can be persuaded and we can get safeguards," he said.

"The idea is that NATO is supposed to be able to fight a war in Europe without using its nuclear weapons right away, is that it? What about that? They can do that better now than eight years ago, I suppose," said a journalist.

"We have made a very substantial increase of conventional capability for defense in this theater and I think we have adherence to the theory of sensible nonnuclear force to make the nonnuclear option viable up to a sensible level of destruction.

"Our program together with that of the Germans remains as it has always been, directed toward the ultimate desire of reunification but excluding absolutely pressure by the East. We and NATO and the Germans are estimating the possibility of disengagement and accommodation of the interests of all parties. We are looking for a positive repermutation of forces of Moscow and the East and with the right disposition the emergence of a new political unit would be simple and peaceful and in the course of things," he said.

"What do you want to say about Czechoslovakia?" said a journalist.

"There is a dynamism at work in the East and in Moscow as well, a non-ideological nationalism raising itself and feeling toward liberalism as we interpret it in a human sense and we see a great deal more confidence and real threat to power centers and the appropriate tack for us is certainly to promote this even when we have the weight of descending reactive forces of Russian tanks.

"We can interpret the move against Czechoslovakia as a check but it must be understood as a major counterforce to Soviet consolidation of its prospectus for the East and as representing the direction of progress which has been set back as to the time scale but proceeds slowly with impediments and the dissatisfaction of the population," he said.

"What would you like to say about the Middle East?" said a journalist.

"In these countries we see the possibility of modification of the power equation with the Soviet to the extent where we can expect a dove-tailing of aims with the rest of Europe, and a wide concert in Europe and reconciliation. I foresee a very productive period with the European countries and Britain associated with them and a new mutual effort that will come with awareness of benefits of teamwork and harmony with just division of authority and the United States will be very happy with this and maintain helpful cordiality with Europe.

"In the Middle East now the moves are not attached to the two powers but the indigenous structures and it implies a disposition they regard as equitable with attention to the knots of pride and honor and with a guarantee that it will be surrounded by a region supplying by treaty recognition and removal of formal and de facto belligerency.

"Here I am basically optimistic. The only direction toward resolution will be taken when we have realization that settlement is the only practicable thing without prohibitive disruption and I think we will see a rising commitment to a pacific scheme and address to development and I believe the drift of the leaders' opinions is more along this line that it was a year ago and so I have a good deal of hope.

"Of course this is one of the top unresolveds that the new people will have to operate on and there has to be recognition that in the time we had and under the parameters obtaining we were unable to apply the quotient of influence at our disposal and get something like the outcome we would like to see evolve. There must be a sense of the impossibility of two-power dictation even though we can talk and bring pressures to bear but it all remains a function of commitment to nonmilitary action and acceptance that the only realistic recipe for them is peace and starting up on the economic area," he said.

"What are some of the other problems?" said a journalist.

"As to the African sector we have made some very measurable headway, cooperating patiently with the nationalist forces, contacting these people in the United Nations, giving some explicit demonstrations of confidence in their ability to efficiently head up their own institutions and encouraging the governments into regionalism and subregionalism and I think that very soon you will see these places begin to take off industrially," he said.

"We'll have to have something about Viet Nam," said a journalist.

"In southern Africa of course there is still the white-black contretemps as a very probable setup for a radical upburst and we have high likelihood this is going to require attention by the people coming in in the next four years or within the decade and this is one circumstance we have not been able to displace any detectable distance.

"Now about Asia we should have a background awareness of the array of protagonists, focusing on the broken '54 agreements and when President Eisenhower told Kennedy when he was President-elect that the health of Laos in the military and government was very pessimistic and there was even or higher probability of having to establish a ground-based presence in Southeast Asia to save it.

"Now we did some very tough work and in '62 we got a reasonably good Laos treaty with provisions that proscribed presence of outside personnel by all participants and ruling out Hanoi transiting the area with an informal side protocol with Moscow to insure Hanoi compliance but Khrushchev did not carry out his side.

"Looking back at it now we can see there were some adjustments that perhaps would have given things a more favorable tilt and precluded some of the later complications and I think perhaps the miscalculation of the greatest weight was at the end of '62 when you had the treaty supposedly becoming operational and we had proof Hanoi was in there and we neglected to bring it to the attention more decisively of these powers that it was to be rigidly understood that these understandings were to be unequivocally adhered to if there was not to be further diplomatic and military concern.

"Now we are passing into a stage where we can optimistically look for another document on this region and perhaps something on missiles and I have extracted this from these eight years at the highest level and also my government work since the war, that once we have written pledges by the other side we should be most persistent in insuring there are no broaches," he said.

"You must have seen the communist break twenty treaties in that time," said a journalist.

"The crucial point is to get those people in the area with affected interests involved in a settlement and impress the necessity of stability and strict observance and this means Asian participation and multilateral combination in enforcement and in the policing agencies," he said.

"They'll include something about Laos if they ever sign a new peace treaty, is that right? I mean, you would recommend that if you weren't leaving and were working for Nixon when this happens?" said a journalist.

"A war settlement is absolutely contingent on a Laos understanding. There can be no question," he said.

"Do you want to put in a comment about the Harvard affair?" said a journalist.

"I don't know what you're talking about," he said.

"Well, of course the story they've published nearly everywhere that Harvard refused to reinstate you because they were afraid of the anti-war people there rioting or disrupting and the story that the other Ivy schools weren't going to put you on the faculty for the same reason," said one of the journalists.

"No, I had no intention of ever returning to Harvard. After I took a leave of absence in '60 they inquired in '62 whether I intended to return then and I told them at that time that I did not and this was a surrender of my tenure there which I understood perfectly well as two years is the strict maximum for absences as Galbraith demonstrated when he came back from India to go back in," he said.

But they could make exceptions for people very near the top, couldn't they?" said a journalist.

"No exceptions. They make no exceptions whatever. It's a rule and that's it," he said.

"How is another treaty going to work out any better than the treaty on Laos?" said a journalist.

"There were certain contingencies that we didn't pursue at the time, failing on the whole to exploit the total diplomatic spectrum and the lineup of contenders then being rather propitious from our point of view we might have stepped up the provisions we took later," he said.

"Why didn't you do that?" said a journalist.

"This decision was not made at the time. Perhaps there was a certain failure to crystalize our reaction," he said.

"You wanted to send the army into Laos and try to clear it up that way, was that what you told Kennedy?" said a journalist.

"There was very definitely this military contingency and I think the result would have been quite different if our timing had been better considered and it would not have been necessary to put in the massive infusion and bother with all the consequences that came from that," he said.

"Somehow I would think Texas wouldn't agree very much with you," said a journalist.

"You would be mistaken. My position with the Johnson Library will be very demanding and a very great challenge and there will be some very great historical work done and I am very pleased to be one of those chosen to help work up some of these materials. I imagine there will be some books revealing a large amount that has not been covered and I think the display of the facts will shed a different point of view on these events and perhaps some people will be forced to a reassessment," he said.

"How would you land an army in Laos? It's a land-locked country, isn't it? You mean you'd airlift them in? Did they have landing fields and enough airplanes to do that then?" said a journalist.

"We wouldn't have put anyone into Laos, but if we had evidenced some land presence in the adjacent region and generally treated observance of the '62 understanding with far greater deliberation instead of holding off until the near-dissolution in '65 we would be in a better resultant state," he said.

"But Kennedy refused you?" said a journalist.

"I don't want to comment on specific occurrences between us at a particular moment. I'll excise this question on the draft," he said.

"I suppose he was still shaken up by his Cuban mess. Did he tell you that was it, he didn't want to do anything after Cuba?" said a journalist.

"I see no point in being specific with that either and I'll take it out. I don't want to put my memoirs in the newspaper. I'll get this sort of thing in the books I'll do and I have in mind a general policy review in historical terms from my vantage point and an analysis and recommendations for the future," he said.

"Kennedy must have seen, though, we would either be involved or not and he would have to decide immediately because those governments would either stand or not. Is that what you told him?" said a journalist.

"We always have to grapple with the pervading bent of our sort of apparatus which has always been historically true of wariness of foreign action until the crisis breaks and we have no choice so there is considerable wavering and too often no steady direction in the foreign field. There is preoccupation with domestic questions and great hesitancy when it comes to circumstances with the implication of deploying the military," he said.

There was a knock at the door of the room. A man came into the room.

"His office is on the phone now. Do you want me to put him on?" said the man.

"Put him on two," he said.

"I'm not beating around with this. This is an attack against me personally that supersedes policy views. I expect you are going to admit a mistake or put in a clarification next month. The entire tone is insulting and outrageous and quite unacceptable. What makes you think you can get off with a thing like that? You have all your facts wrong. Who is this? Why didn't you say so? Put him on. Where is he? Then put him on. I have nothing to say to you. Put him on. Put him on. Rob, come in here," he said.

The man came into the room.

"He's standing there but he refuses to talk to me. He's telling one of his men what to say to me. Take the phone and tell him I want to know what he intends to do about it," he said.

"He wants to know what he intends to do about it," said the man.

"He told him to say he has confidence in his facts," said the man.

"Tell him at least I expect a piece like this to be submitted to me as a courtesy," he said.

"He says at least he expects a piece like that to be submitted to him as a courtesy," said the man.

"He told him to say he doesn't agree with you," said the man.

"Tell him he'd better start using his brains," he said.

"He says for him to start using his brains," said the man.

"He told him to say he doesn't agree with you," said the man.

"What did he say?" he said.

"He said for you to fuck yourself," said the man.

"Tell him I want a retraction he's going to put in. Tell him I want it on my desk by tomorrow," he said.

"He says he wants a retraction on his desk by tomorrow," said the man.

"He said for you to fuck yourself," said the man.

"Tell the son of a bitch to think again. Tell him he better think what the hell he's doing. Tell him he's going to lie in the bed he's making," he said.

"He says he better think again and think what the hell he's doing and he's making a bed and he's going to have to lie in it," said the man.

"He said the same thing," said the man.

"Hang up. Get me Political Affairs at State," he said.

"I saw that article. He did a bad knife job on you, didn't he?" said a journalist.

"These are propositions of hindsight but we should keep some of our attention to understand that when President Johnson responded and injected higher levels in '65 we see the beginning of some very favorable side effects, the economic and social pictures showing real upswings and some political fallout that is completely unique in history, the beginnings of cooperation and regionalism among the countries and I think as of our going out in January '69 we have an Asia with several bright indicators for the future and if we stay steady and if they stay steady we will have the possibility of gradual retrenchment with avoidance of isolationism and successful transfer of responsibility to the GVN and formation of a partnership with us in the junior role in many regards," he said.

There was a knock at the door of the room. The man came into the room.

"I've got Political Affairs if you want to talk now," said the man.

"Two," he said.

"Is this Davies? Good morning. About this thing they've got up against me in the *Bulletin*, you've read it, haven't you? This man is on your chart, am I right? I've never come across him before. Well, what kind of a folder are you giving him? He refuses to listen when I talk to him. I think the thing would be to input this obvious slander against a man as a vector in his performance scores matrix. I know about those people over there but couldn't you have moved to head this thing off or give me some heads up? I know he's not thinking about staying on because I know Rogers' men. No. This is stronger. This man has sought to ridicule me. I'll be looking for something and I think you have seen a good deal from me and I hope this will be the result. Well, I'll talk to you later about it. Yes. Good-by," he said.

"Do you want to say anything about Canada and Trudeau?" said a journalist.

"There's nothing there that is major for me to set out and let me fit China into the picture of general policy and say that there is no point of contradiction here with this country, we have no subdesigns in relation to it and there is no inherent justification for the present irrational rigidity and xenophobia and no explanation except when we have taken preventive action against aggressive acts against near-distant constitutional governments and elsewhere and we have spelled out our willingness to apply a different interpretation of our mutual roles if we are given some signal it is willing to conduct itself in a new role.

"This has yet to occur and President Johnson has extended himself as far as possible to make this assurance but we have yet to sense the appreciation of the other side that must come soon that an out from its dilemmas can only be contemplated on the basis of internal restructuring, attention to efficiency, serious production designs. So we have not been able to normalize with them and we are waiting for the mainland to bring itself into accord with the protocols of diplomacy and restrict its ambitions behind its boundaries. For this I think we will just have to await a thorough rethinking of strategy by the primary leadership circle, probably also elimination of Mao and his anti-rational prejudices against us.

"Bob, come in here," he said.

The man came into the room.

"Do you know this man? What do you know about his plans?" he said.

"I think for a while he worked for Time-Life. I think I've heard something about him going to *Look* now. I don't know much about him," said the man.

"Get me Rafferty at *Look*," he said.

"What's going to happen with the United States not long ago bringing home some troops from Germany to save money and then if we have a treaty bringing back troops from Southeast Asia? Are the Russians going to move in?" said a journalist.

"We have only been drawing back marginally in Germany with two brigades of the Twenty-Fourth Division in this country set to quick-reaction reinforce and you won't see a sharp fadeout of our position in Asia and our security situation will be identical because by this time we will have the giant planes. You will see forward-siting of the heavy equipments and the troops and planes on alert and requiring minimum time-lapse for injection.

"We can see that most of the doubtful areas will be covered under this theory—Asia, the Middle East, Africa, Europe, where we will have the guarded equipment bases and the suitable synchronicity with the host country with their desire present for the plan, all this of course being provisions for the future since we have now only one or two C-5's, and this is the tendency of our thinking into the seventies and I think you will see this program ripen as the time comes," he said.

There was a knock at the door of the room. The man came into the room.

"I've got Rafferty if you want me to put him through now," said the man.

"Two," he said.

"Yes, Hello. Very well. Yes. Have you ever come across a man named Brady? No. Yes. That's the one. Yes. Good. Has he been in there about a position after the twentieth? Maybe another man there has talked to him. He worked for Time-Life. Is that so? I didn't know that. I don't go there. No, I've never met him. He has not spoken to me. I am not acting for anyone. I don't know anything about his plans. That's all right. Good-by. Thank you," he said.

"These are the various specifics which have held the efforts of President Johnson and I think with everything in the balance there has been a decided gain in the positive dimension but I think probably what will prove to be the largest plus factor that will loom larger in the future when it is evaluated will be the push that the President has made to cut off in the foreign policy discussion the dichotomy between isolationism and the involvement that because of our recent experience some people have calculated as going beyond the appropriate response and this has not entered into analysis because of the war issue.

"The fact is since he set out with it in '66 he has put a good deal of effort into precluding a destructive contention between the voices of isolation and foreign responsibilities, dealing not in rhetoric and theory but executing elements of policy passing between the two doctrines. You saw in New Orleans the President unveil a plan of cooperation, replacing the former dependence with shared burden and partnership and a fair distribution of responsibility and effected by steps in the areas of the monetary management, trade and aid and the concrete groundwork of regionalism in many different quarters of the globe," he said.

"You talk about the different policies you want the Russians and the rest of the communists to take on these questions but do you think they are really going to change? What are we going to do if they don't? And what changes do you think the United States should make in the future?" said a journalist.

"We have in the Middle East opinions where there will have to be a good deal of modification among the small powers and while it is true that it is not in our capacity to initiate movement we still retain a good deal of persuasion and we can perform with it and we are performing and as for Russian initiatives I think we have to hope for the emergence of a more rational approach," he said.

"Do you have anything you'd like to say to all the people who criticized you and said you were to blame for the war with this supposedly dividing the country and Johnson offering to bow out and what do you think of the demonstrators?' said a journalist.

"Here there is merely outgrowths of the normal functioning of our practice. This is democracy and these are anticipatable effusions and eruptions which have been evidenced in every time except for an audible level of these voices which we have not met with since before the first war and I think we can be satisfied that this is healthy and shows attention to our overseas role and enlarges the governmental process and the future will bring a great deal more placidity as the forces in Asia and our efforts are fully measured and personality discounted. As for demonstrations, it is a method of pageantry that I don't think anyone could dispute and I think everyone has a feeling for the excitement of these sorts of political drives.

"Bob, call up someone about this man," he said.

"As for China our hands are tied by their paralysis and there is no recourse to pry them from this syndrome if they don't make some indication and we have exercised a lot of creative thought in signaling our readiness to adopt new contacts and exchanges but there has not been a nibble. There can be progress here at any time but I don't see how this can come until the policy-makers clarify their own minds and communicate it," he said.

"What do you say about Russian power compared to ours? What about the Russian navy in the Mediterranean and they've supposedly quadrupled their land missiles in two years. What happens when they catch up in in power?" said a journalist.

"The balance is not shifting to the East. At the same time there must be constant scrutiny and innovation to insure there will be no change that will provide an invitation to eager foreign leadership. This implies no radical abdication of our interest in Europe, the Middle East, Asia, because as far ahead as we can plot we will constitute the deciding edge in the international pattern because of our nuclear status and commitments and our trade and our commercial activities and political authority and I think if we are steady as we proceed we can look for substantial development toward what President Johnson has outlined as an international blueprint of cooperation and just material shares," he said.

There was a knock at the door of the room. The man came into the room.

"It seems he's quite well known. He's a lawyer but he doesn't practice. He's been in HEW and several places at State. Everyone is supposed to like him and he's from California.

Some people think he's expecting to stay. Evidently he works in the government as a kind of hobby. He's got holdings of thirty-two million dollars in Control Data," said the man.

"Thank you," he said.

"We should be very alert to the hazards of the urge of precipitous drawback because we have several powers very willing to fill out into vacuums and probe soft spots and upset weak alliances and these powers will continue but we do not look for the gray areas around the world to be filled out with American manpower but by locals that have been sufficiently stiffened materially and politically although there will not be zero probability of disposing units into certain points.

"I would strongly discourage any concept of repudiating our security agreements and assuming the fortress mode but rather expect to be able to carry through our affairs and obligations in concert with other power units and we will be able to distribute the weight of this work. This diffusion to an extent of leadership is not a sore point, we have seen it evolve gradually since after the war and '47 when we began with the Marshall idea of European reconstitution even if this entailed the bolstering of forces and a certain risk of another vortex of forces and a certain risk because we held to the hypothesis that our interests would be in phase despite any friction," he said.

"Bob, come in here and open a window. My God, it's hot in here," he said.

The man came into the room. The man opened a window of the room.

"Crack the door as you go out," he said.

"So on the one hand you have this European approach of unification and on the other you have President Johnson as he pressed for Latin American integration, the Central American common market, aid, economic and political coordination and these are two sides of the same impulse.

This is the natural path of our policy, not thinking of clients but generating a cooperative aura and we should continue to channel this forward because this should be the cast of our policy contingencies.

"Bob, crack the door. I think I told you to keep the door cracked. I think you can see the draft has pretty much closed the door.

"We have not yet entirely erased the specter of cataclysm but we have advanced and set the wheels in motion with the peace talks and looming missile talks. We can be confident I think of a world in rising harmony with a slight scaledown of American bustle and an appreciation of mutual effort and cooperation in which all the countries will have a just voice and the people of the world will move equitably into abundance and you will see respect and dignity and consideration in a democratic setting on most every side.

"Bob, crack the door, dammit," he said.

ELEVEN

THE ATTACK

In those days we were at a fire support base in the Highlands. One night they attacked and we kept firing. There were lots and lots of white flares and green tracers. They were rather spectacular and we watched them. We were in a trench behind the wire. A sergeant behind us said he would shoot any of us who did not stay in the trench. I had a whole crate of ammunition. I was quite sure I was going to die. There were two hundred of them. I thought, so this was it, it all came to this. I thought, so this was to be the sum of my existence. I was just to stand there in a trench in Asia and shoot men until they overran us for the sake of this sergeant. I thought about all those days I had spent in schools studying about things. It was amusing. I thought it was rather ridiculous. They killed nearly everyone at the fire base. There were twenty of us there that night. I was not wounded at all. They did not kill the sergeant. They never do in real life, you know.

A VERY SPLENDID VICTORY

The Capture of the Village of Chanh Luu,
Viet Nam, 9 August 1968

Oh yea, yes indeed, great heroes we were in those days. We won a splendid victory one weekend in those days, a very splendid victory. We captured the village of Chanh Luu. We captured the village of Chanh Luu again. We captured the village of Chanh Luu every few weeks and every few weeks we won a very splendid victory. The peasants of the village of Chanh Luu were very stubborn and they were very wrong-headed so it was necessary for us to win a great victory and a great victory every few weeks.

Chanh Luu was twenty-five miles north of Saigon. Six thousand peasants lived there. It was a tidy and prosperous village. The peasants of Chanh Luu were very stubborn and were sympathetic to the Viet Cong. Our officers told us they did not know why the peasants of Chanh Luu were sympathetic to the Viet Cong. Our officers told us the peasants were sympathetic to the Viet Cong even though American medical teams had treated them for several years. Also Government propaganda teams had given them supplies and leaflets. Our officers told us Government security teams had gone to Chanh Luu but had been forced to leave after a few weeks. The Viet Cong had menaced the village from Zone D to the east. Now it was necessary for the Government to draft many peasants from Chanh Luu and for Government soldiers to shoot at houses in Chanh Luu when they attacked the village and for us to capture the village of Chanh Luu and capture the village of Chanh Luu every few weeks and to win a very splendid victory every few weeks.

It was a very splendid battle. The Eleventh Armored Regiment surrounded the village with sixty-seven tanks and armored personnel carriers. Machine-gunners fired a great deal of ammunition across fields when they believed they saw enemy soldiers. Battalions of the Fifth Division of the Government entered the village. The Government soldiers fired a great deal of ammunition. They killed eighteen men. A few shots were fired from the village. A few Government soldiers were wounded. The Government soldiers captured a hundred and thirty-two prisoners. The prisoners were discovered hiding in holes in the floor, under beds and in bathrooms and in holes in banana groves. After the firing had ceased our officers entered the village and walked in the market place. Our officers were very pleased with the result of the battle and believed the victory to be the result of their sound military strategy.

Peasants of the village squatted on their heels in the market place. They looked at us and our officers and the Government soldiers. We heard Government soldiers beating a man in the back room of a stucco house. Our officers stood watching Government soldiers pile rifles and grenades in the center of the market place. The rifles and grenades were rifles and grenades that had been discovered in the possession of peasants of the village. A Government soldier pushed an old man into the village square. There was mud in the old man's hair. The old man's daughter was tied to him by a rope. Men and women peasants with their hands tied crouched in rows in an open storehouse. There was mud on some of the peasants. Other peasants were wet and pale. Government soldiers had tortured them by forcing them to swallow large amounts of water. The peasants were silent. The other peasants were silent when a peasant woman cried out. She had recognized her husband. A Government soldier was leading her husband into the village square. Our officers looked at the pile of rifles and grenades in the center of the market place. Government soldiers piled the rifles and grenades in the marketplace. Our officers displayed great interest in the pile of rifles and grenades in the marketplace.

There were signs on buildings in the village. The signs were printed neatly in English. The signs read, "Stop terrorist raids. Lay down your arms. Cross to our side. You will be safely repatriated." The signs had been painted by members of the Viet Cong. Our officers looked at the signs and smiled. Our officers swaggered about with their hands on their hips. One of our officers was General Abrams. He had flown from Saigon in a helicopter to observe the attack. General Abrams wore a baseball cap and carried a bone-handled revolver and smoked a cigar. Another officer was Colonel George Patton. Colonel George Patton was the commander of the Eleventh Armored Regiment and wore a tanker's helmet and a bullet-proof vest. He too smoked a cigar. He was the son of the hero of World War Two. Other officers told him he had again fought creditably in battle in the manner of his father. Our officers congratulated each other for their actions during the attack. It had been a very splendid attack and a significant victory. A colonel admitted it would be necessary to attack the village again in a few weeks.

"It's sanitized until we leave. Then it's unsanitized," said the colonel.

Some of our officers believed the village of Chanh Luu ought to be destroyed. They believed the village ought to be destroyed and the peasants in it moved to a secure area in the manner of the village of Bien Suc in January 1967.

"I can't argue with the philosophy you shouldn't keep destroying villages. But when you consistently take casualties it becomes a moot point," said an officer.

There were photographers in the village. The photographers had entered the village with our officers. Our officers posed for the photographers. Our officers shook hands and smiled, posing for the photographers. The peasants looked at our officers posing for the photographers. The peasants were silent. Our officers told us they were proud of our actions during the battle. We had conducted ourselves with bravery, very splendid bravery. There had been no American casualties in the battle. One of our officers had inadvertently touched the barrel of a machine-gun. He had burned his hand. He refused medical treatment for his injury. He said it was nothing, nothing at all.

TWELVE

THE WEAPON

The colonel smoked a long cigar. The colonel wore an Australian bush hat and a blue scarf. In the helicopter the colonel talked into a headset and looked at a map. The helicopter flew over the swamp.

"I got the hat from a friend over with the Australians at Nui Dat," the colonel said to a reporter. "It's a damn sharp hat, don't you think?"

Near the door of the helicopter the specialist watched the dial of an instrument.

"It's a tremendous weapon," said the colonel. "Out here we call it the people sniffer. They've been experimenting around with it for about a year but they sent us the new model here. It picks up the ammonia smell or something of sweat people give off. It works like a charm. In the Mekong Delta here we figure it's the best thing since women.

"You see, here it's flat with not many trees and you can observe. You can't use it so well in the jungle. If you can't spot them or their emplacement the smell could be from somewhere they just left. And in the jungle and the mountains you can't bring in people to engage them quickly like you can here."

The helicopter skimmed ten feet above the swamp. The needle on the dial of the instrument pointed at the maximum value. The specialist threw a grenade out the door of the helicopter. The grenade began to release a stream of red smoke. The colonel pointed at mud walls camouflaged with brush.

"Those are VC bunkers. That's a marking grenade. There's a helicopter behind us. It'll watch for movement if they try to get away. It can get them with miniguns. There's an infantry company about a mile from here. We'll call them in."

"There're a lot of people in that bunker or there were recently, very recently," said the specialist. "This is a pretty accurate instrument."

"Sometimes when we get a reading we shoot up to a thousand feet, and drop out tear gas," said the colonel. "It comes in a big container that scatters two hundred and sixty four little tear gas canisters. They're about the size of flashlight batteries. It covers an area the size of a football field. The gas gets them to move around and the second helicopter can observe and we can seal off the area. It's too windy today. When it's windy the gas disperses too quickly.

"Last Monday in Long An Province here the sniffer helped my brigade pinpoint the position of two companies. We surrounded the area and got a hundred and four dead by actual body count. It was one of the most successful engagements of the war during the week.

"We'll orbit around the bunkers for a while so you can see our boys clear them out. It'll take them a few minutes to get here."

The colonel talked into the headset and looked at the swamp.

Soon soldiers appeared near the bunkers. They fired automatic rifles, machine-guns and rockets at the bunkers. After a while they ceased firing.

The colonel talked into the headset. The colonel frowned.

"I guess the bunkers were empty," said the colonel. "You see, all animals give off this ammonia smell, dead animals too. I guess what it was, near the bunkers there they found a dead pig."

THE UNDER SECRETARY

I'm not saying I'm a hero exactly but the victory was very, very key and it will figure very, very large in the history when it is written, and it was damn tricky but you got to say we pulled it off in the end and the thing was we never know dick how it would go till the very end and we make a move and they make a countermove and if we get beat up on we just dust ourselves off and jump right back into the fight and it is real touch and go there for a while, believe me, but we come out on top because we never give in and we never give up and we never let up and we put our heads down and keep driving ahead and it looks pretty bleak till practically the last minute and we are pretty well holding our breaths but we know we are closer and closer to winning because our tactical and strategic positions are steadily improving slowly but surely and more and more guys are coming over to our side but, still, everything depends on Lyndon because we don't know what kind of shit Lyndon might pull but then you have the showdown the last week of March and we have to scramble but Rusk—we call him Mister Potato Head not only because of the way he looks if you get my drift—is always the guy we have to go up against in the Department and he knows we're entrenched there and he knows he can't clear us all out and he's laying down some very serious suppressive fire.

And he thinks his top echelon is a hundred per cent behind him—wrong again—but any time he goes over and does a consult with Lyndon he surrounds himself with a cadre of loyalist ass-kissers, and our guys can't break out but we're underground there and steady sapping their defenses and we break into some reports and position papers and sometimes we slip in some dissenting viewpoints but mostly we're aggregating our strength and anticipating breaks in Rusk's front because with money flowing like piss and getting just about zilch to show for it we know they're bound to come and also we're coordinating with guys outside the Department, guys near Lyndon, also in DOD, to maneuver jointly and you'll be damned surprised when I tell you frankly there were even guys with us very, very close to the Joint Chiefs and so we are always probing for soft spots but let me tell you fall '67 is bad for us and we have to endure multiple boat-loads of crap in the military and political evaluations but we know it can't last because we know the reality is the war isn't going that well because we know any kind of adequate program on the political side is AWOL plus we know these graphs and computer indicators aren't worth a dry fart but rebuttal is useless because reason is not part of the argument, and so then you have McNamara's press briefing at the end of November where he announces in the near future—and this is weird: he doesn't state a date certain—I guess he doesn't have the World Bank gig quite lined up yet—he'll be packing it in.

Which is a big defeat for us because we've maintained a conduit to him for longer than I'm going to reveal, finally achieving success when he writes Lyndon a memo coming out against more troops and continuing the bombing of the North and so for which here is Lyndon cutting off his legs at the knees, and so then you have the Tet Offensive, which rattles all the cups in everybody's cupboard, doubt you not, with Lyndon knocked for a loop and landing on his ass or his elbow, he knows not which. He can't figure it—he thought he had just about nailed all the VC skins to the wall and bombed the shit out of the NVA and here is fighting all up and down the country and all over the place and he has to contend with the monster media play with its mostly negative slant—a PR disaster—and Lyndon yells why didn't somebody tell me something like this is going to hit the fan and he's demanding to know why all those intelligence reports and captured documents and computer-generated projections didn't predict it and so Lyndon is a mite perturbed and says to everybody in sight the North Vietnamese will get away with this over his dead body and so on and so forth and generally doing his usual imitation of Sam Houston at San Jacinto. Just about everybody but Joe Alsop is going to concede the VC and NVA are showing more than we thought they had and they are thinking about doing some rethinking of strategy but this does not include Lyndon and so what does he do—if you can believe—he tells Wheeler to go over and ask Westy what he wants, what size force—reinforcements—he thinks he should have, which to say the least is not the path of wisdom since with regard to Westy I'm not going to go into the matter of how acute that fellow is because I think that matter is pretty well established in everyone's mind. He doesn't know what the hell is going on at this point with all his printouts way up and his body counts way up and the number of strategic hamlets way up and all the sudden all hell breaking loose up, down, here, there and everywhere and listen to this: he comes up with this: he needs immediate large-scale reinforcements so Saigon doesn't fall, which of course is prime bull because Saigon isn't going to fall any more that Washington, DC is going to fall or Syracuse, New York is going to fall.

Westy says he needs five divisions and their support and he argues like this if you can call it an argument: the VC have taken big casualties and are pretty weak and he should have more men in there to take advantage and this is going to shorten the length of the conflict and he's got to have insurance in Saigon, Hue and other places in case they reinforce because his men are off balance and Wheeler buys this and they add it up and come up with two hundred and six thousand and so then you have on 28 February Wheeler flies back in a rush with this in his briefcase and he briefs Lyndon and a few of Lyndon's men and then the cabinet—whipping out maps and graphs and stats and throwing around much bunk, with Lyndon nodding yes and yes. And right away in go two brigades, airborne, by airlift, ten thousand, and Lyndon's hot to trot like the commies are personally insulting his manhood and he's all for tossing the two hundred thousand in there right away, so you would have five hundred thirty, thirty-five thousand already authorized for Viet Nam with this making a real big per cent add-on but at first Lyndon couldn't care less about that: he is talking about sticking a million in there and giving Ho's beard a yank—a real Yankee yank.

It surprises me not at all and I just figure we're down one but, you see—guess what?—there's a catch to it, because Lyndon can't just whip out another two hundred thousand like he's done before because he's got nowhere to come up with them and he's either got to raise the draft way up or start in on the reserves and those are two things I think you'll agree that wouldn't sit too good with a lot of people of standing and influence and Lyndon sort of gradualed into this war and slipped into it on the quiet and it would be very difficult to start in now on mobilization and controls on the economy but still Lyndon charges ahead and they tell him nope, it just can't be done without stretching out deployment. This is something for our side—maybe we can delay deployments and whittle the numbers down plus you've got to figure in the political picture with the primaries coming up the next month and all those demonstrations against Lyndon, which he is really quite thin-skinned about, oddly enough, and here is Westy also saying to finish this thing off he needs to go into Cambodia and Laos to go after their bases and as much as Lyndon would give his left nut to get this thing over with he knows in no way does he want to touch the domestic and foreign politics of publicly doing these things and he is at least smart enough to nix that because we really wouldn't expect him to go with that one but you never really know what's going to bubble up out of the manhole with Lyndon and so what comes down at this point is that Lyndon says he wants to set up a review to review what to do, which we know of course is just his way of trying to find a way of reinforcing under the radar but at any rate it's something we on our part see as a plus since it has to mean delay and Lyndon tells Clifford to head up a review panel— Clifford who wasn't in yet as McNamara's successor—he was going to get sworn in the next day, March first, and we didn't think much of this guy.

He's we know of course a champeen influence peddler and lobbyist—I don't know, maybe he's a bag man—you know a lot of them are—and the rap is he's the guy with absolutely the best connections of anybody in the entire town, and he was in the Navy during the war as some Admiral's executive secretary or executive officer or something like that and he's been figured for a hard-liner dating from way back when and so we figure we can't get anywhere near him anything like with McNamara and so we figured we'd have to work around him and maybe try to get in with someone or some two guys close in around Lyndon and we were actually feeling a bit optimistic even after the McNamara disaster that we could at least chip away at the troop numbers and maybe even do more because you see this was the time when you had Congress in a royal dudgeon about expenditures and you had the gold market mess then too and the new troop package would have upset the balance of payments too besides tacking on ten, twelve billion to the present thirty billion number, which would have been hairy because Lyndon's got most people thinking it's costing less than thirty and so he's got his staff working overtime to make sure the papers on this troop business don't get out and threatening to circumcise anybody they found out leaked it, especially to the press, but this is too big.

They can't sit on something as big as this. Mr. Potato Head—we call him Freckles, also—doesn't let anything circulate outside his office but like I said we already know what was coming down and just to show you we also got tips from some DOD assistant secretary staff people and a couple colonels and even one general—indeedy they were coming in thick and fast and this gets our morale up even a little more since of course it means our alliances are multiplying fast whereas on the other hand there are Pentagon types who figure that if this gets out it's going to make them look pretty darn silly, like with half a million grunts over there plus huge navy and air the other side with next to zero navy and little air is whipping our ass but you also had the more considered civilian and uniform types like I mentioned who'd gone through the '65 bit with Lyndon slipping a couple hundred thousand over there on the sly before almost anybody was the wiser and who want to get the word out in time this time to get up some telling pressure against him. A number of the wiser among the empowered class at this point actually begin to try to think this war business through and they just couldn't come up with a likely scenario for victory following Lyndon's lead. The trust factor was beginning to erode. Myself, I couldn't make a move to leak since they were starting to be on to me—I'd placed stuff with *Times* people on the real cost of the war—and had to be careful to stay strictly under camouflage so we went far enough down in the Department to a couple civil servants we could trust who wouldn't be suspected and couldn't be connected to us and there you are, and so you had real heat brought to bear this time as I'm sure you remember—uproar, objections on all sides. Lyndon is very, very, very pissed. Believe you me.

He howls at everybody in the White House demanding they tell him who leaked but natch nobody there is in the know and Lyndon says he's got a traitor on the payroll and says the press is out to get him and, you know, truth be told there were even guys close around Lyndon who thought this escalation business if it went through would end very badly for him and everybody else but of course could say nothing if they valued their family jewels, and we figured since reason did not apply money was the only argument we could use against it and hey, money is a telling lever, ain't it now? so in the afternoon the next day after he's sworn in in the morning Clifford convenes his review panel in his private dining room in the Pentagon and there are a couple guys there who've got some leanings in our direction but the rest are the same guys that have run over us before and who's to say it will be any different this time and we figure this is pretty much just to hammer out the technicalities of getting them over without mobilization, so Potato Head and Rostow are there, Wheeler is there, Maxwell Taylor is there—he's very, very hawky, "special advisor on the war," though of course if you were to ask me I'd tell you he just is not that special—there is Helms, CIA, there is Fowler of Treasury, of course, money being the focus, Nitze and Warnke in DOD—moving a bit more our way, Katzenbach from the Department, William Bundy is coming around some to us, and Phil Goulding from DOD is kind of soft, but expecting the worst as we were this meeting is genuinely surprising when I hear about it: they go more into overall policy and strategy than I expected and there are a few ideas tossed back and forth that actually contain a germ of rationality and reality in the face of which here is Westy holding out for the two hundred thousand by 30 June '69 with a hundred thousand immediately from the actives in the States and increments of fifty thousand from the reserves and Wheeler says with this he can provide victory and it will cut down on the time frame to a very reasonable period but when they press him he guarantees nothing and won't fix a date—it's the same slop he's been tossing to people for eight straight years—and it so happens that there was a research paper a couple of analytical types with us at the CIA had put together—yes, it's a fact we had guys even in the CIA—this paper was an analysis of the likely sequela of escalation with a ton of facts and figures—uncommitted troops of the NVA, realistic estimated rate of losses, rate of replacement from the population pool, real effects of the bombing, supply to the NVA from China and the Soviet Union, etcetera etcetera, the bottom line being the result would be just a mutual escalation without a determinative effect on outcome, and Warnke had rescued this from the wastebasket a couple of times and here he is presenting the data to the brassies, who weren't too receptive as you might imagine, but he proceeds anyway to put out the idea of deescalation, the end of search and destroy and withdrawal from Khe Sanh and the other isolated firebases and mobile shields around the cities and buildup of the Arvin—which as you might imagine didn't impress the brassies either in the least, having heard the same many times before and having easily fended it off without much effort.

I imagine at this point they are worried not at all. One would predict that Warnke wouldn't make a quick piss's worth of difference, as cogent as his arguments are to the normal person, but Clifford, strangely, isn't immediately dismissive, maybe due to consciousness of his essential ignorance of the situation militarily and politically at the micro level or maybe even doubts about the conventional narrative and in that simple-seeming and deferential and elegant and super polite way he has he asks the brassies some simple questions—like is this counterinsurgency or conventional war and what happens if the GVN implodes and what happens if this installment isn't enough—and apparently he isn't terribly impressed by the answers he's getting, which is an attitude which is surprising when you consider that this is a guy who came out against the thirty-six day pause in December '65 but on the other hand Lyndon sent him to the Philippines, Thailand, Australia, New Zealand, South Korea to squeeze balls for bigger contributions and he gets nada so I'm sure the guy learned a little something from that, like they've all got their own agendas, which intersect America's only coincidentally—i.e., they're not much seeing themselves as dominos—this is August '67, when they're having secret contacts, which Clifford is OK with, figuring the VC and the North are getting ready to give it up, they have no choice. Lyndon gives out with his San Antonio formula on 30 September '67 for a bombing halt providing we get productive talks and they don't take military advantage, whatever either one of those means, and then more secret messages in January '68 where Clifford figures they're about exhausted in the South and would pull some out for a halt—from all of which you would have to figure Clifford for just another of the sadly deluded who place their faith in Lyndon, and he has his confirmation hearing on 25 January '68 and declares without coordinating with Lyndon that the San Antonio formula is consistent with infiltration from the North so long as it doesn't go up.

Generating a not small firestorm. Mr. Potato throws an unquiet fit—to him infiltration is original sin and he doesn't want a halt until every last man is out of the South and he runs over to Lyndon and hangs on his ear for two days to get him to issue a correction but a couple of our guys caught Lyndon in a hallway and explain there was no way he could contradict a man he had just appointed without making himself look really, really bad, which he ended up buying, and the Department announces this as official policy on 29 January, causing us to grin and chalk one up and causing Potato Face as you may imagine to be pissed big time, so he calls some of us into his office and says he knows some of us have been busy at the White House and we look at each other and frown and shake our heads and say not us—it was funny: we beat him out and he knows it and, man, the bastard was so mad his face was purple as a plum, and so then you have Clifford sends the first summary on his review panel over to Lyndon—this is 5 March—and it went with fifty thousand within three months and a staged schedule for the rest over fifteen months, so this gives us delay but no cut, so if this is adopted we for sure are going to go after more and we are absolutely prepared to launch a campaign but it does show that Clifford won't touch mobilization.

But we're waiting for it to be formally adopted and what happens it doesn't happen—it was clear that Lyndon was holding back: you could tell he was a little bit scared of this one, with the politics, with McCarthy making a solid show in New Hampshire on 1 March, and there was this gold business that might blow up with further unbalancing of the balance of payments and he's starting to receive a lot of noise from a lot of people because if you can imagine there are a lot of weekend soldiers who would like to keep it that way and the party hacks are nervous and Lyndon is not sure, he wants to keep away from it, he doesn't want to get his fingers burnt and Clifford doesn't want to push it and have it hung around his neck if it blows up so he treads water and says the matter merits further review and meanwhile he'll check back with Westy to see if the force mix they've made up for the ten thousand and the rest is okay—purely a ploy to delay, of course—while meanwhile Lyndon is receiving heat from Stennis and Russell in the Senate and Rivers in the House about Westy asking to activate the reserves: they inform him that the reserves are in a total mess. And so then you have things sort of drifted along and we got to thinking with some blood and sweat we might be able to get something on cutting the numbers and Clifford is still meeting with his panel, still discussing, and we have a couple men in the Air Force writing up ideas and Hoopes pitched them to the panel: the bombing isn't doing anything, it costs too much, it's not a fact the casualties would go way up with a halt, the North is just as strong as ever, it isn't efficient or cost effective and so on and so forth.

I started to think about now maybe there's a real possibility we can bend this Clifford guy and I think maybe we might end up pulling it out of the horse's ass after all and about this time I eat lunch with Clifford over at the Senate and a couple of Senators leave the table and I'm talking to him by myself—mano a mano—I've got some kind of paper about some Buddhists Thieu's thrown in jail I'm supposed check out with him—and after a while I work around to strategy and I say whatever the benefits of escalation might be—and they would be few and far between in my opinion—they would be outweighed by the political deficits—in-country and in the US—and the political considerations would be determinative and could very well be disastrous, not to mention the severely negatory diplomatic consequences and the consequences of more debt and worse balance of payments to the financial system and I see that he's listening to what I'm saying—he's pushing his food from one side of the plate to the other—I forget what it was, I think it was rigatoni—so I pile on with you've got to look beyond the strategic details and step back and consider the whole picture: what is the definition of success that you think you are working toward and, two, what is the actual probability of achieving that outcome, given the existing constraints. It should be a matter of logic and probability rather than political passion and he says something like personally he can think of better ways the money could be spent and I'm thinking this guy is more rational than I would ever expect from his record and I am feeling here is a bendable guy and just maybe I have turned this man some and maybe lit a fire under his ass or at least warmed his behind to get him to start drawing the right conclusions and in fact as the days go by we start to hear from our guys that he is making more and more good-sounding noises like pointing to the problems with the National Guard and Army Reserve or the negatives of extending the tour of duty or problems he has with doubling down on troop strength as the only strategy and he's not comfortable with the failure to clearly define the end game.

So it looks like the hard work we've been putting in is starting to pay off and I think you have to say that a good part of this has to be scored to me and we get reports that Clifford is meeting with Lyndon and hasn't been ejected from the room yet so it looks like our team is making gains and we are calculating that if anybody can be a valuable weapon it's Clifford, the two of them being bosom buddies for thirty years, but of course nothing is guaranteed because let me tell you something, trying to persuade Lyndon Johnson is like trying to persuade a cat, and coming up on the middle of March nobody has heard anything—approval, disapproval, or let's forget the matter ever came up—but Rostow is up to his usual malignant maneuvers and tells Lyndon Clifford's got himself taken in by the professional waverers and nervous Nellies and he's been pushing since the end of February for a tough-ass war speech with talking points like the Tet business was nothing bad for the allies, it was a disaster for the commies, the US is going to do whatever is necessary to achieve its objective of letting the Vietnamese decide their own fate and etcetera etcetera until it overflows the john— real blood and thunder stuff; McPherson at the White House is assigned to write it in case Lyndon decides to go that way. He is personally close to us but he tells me he's got no wiggle room to tone things down and we're dreading Lyndon actually decides to deliver this thing and it doesn't look so good and so then you have Goldberg coming into it in the middle of March with a private letter to Lyndon dated 15 March giving reasons for a halt in order to start up negotiations—which I was glad to hear about because I like Goldberg and he is very much with us but I figure with the slot he occupies his sway as an advisor is pretty near to zero—I figure he doesn't have visitation rights to Lyndon, you might put it—and I'm expecting his response will be no response since the buzz has been that he's said that he's heard all the arguments for a halt and he ain't convinced so obviously we had work to do in this regard and we were bound and determined to do it and we just girded our loins again and tried to come up with a new move, but then what happens is Clifford comes up with a proposal, putting it to Lyndon he could narrow down the bombing to below the twentieth parallel. He tells Lyndon Lyndon can say he isn't calling a halt and getting nothing in return and he's not hurting the boys at Khe Sanh, the Rockpile, Camp Carroll—those places up by the DMZ.

He tells him this is sure to make him look good, peace-minded, and it might start momentum toward a deescalation process and with Kennedy announcing for President on 16 March it would pay to come up with some kind of peace initiative, which did seem apparently to get him to thinking from the way he was looking kind of mopy, but the fact was that MacNamara came up with the same or similar proposal in spring '67—moving the bombing below the twentieth or nineteenth—but you had a couple of brassies threatening to resign if Lyndon went along and the Joint Chiefs expressed objections as well but still anyway Lyndon put out overtures to Hanoi but he thinks he got no indication they were interested in dealing and now nobody knows if they would be now, and so then you have Lyndon goes out to Minneapolis and talks to the National Farmers Union—this is 18 March. So my God this is the Rostow speech: he goes on about tucking tail and abandoning commitments and Munich and defense of liberty and he's not going to abandon search and destroy and circle the wagons around the cities resulting in more casualties of innocent women and children, so we have to chalk one up to Rostow and this seems to set us back on our heels after the progress we thought we were making with Clifford but think about it did it that much because the big thing you'll notice is this speech doesn't say anything about troop additions— which is the significant point at issue at this point—so the battle is far from over, and so then Lyndon pulls a surprise. We hear that Goldberg met with Lyndon on the twentieth and to all appearances it was a cordial exchange of views, with Lyndon listening to what he has got to say and asking a few questions about his position and asking him to come and state his position at a meeting of his wise men he's calling for the twenty-fifth, the meeting of the wise men being at Clifford's instigation as he knew there was a meeting of the wise men in November '67 when they all went with a full court press but the situation is very different now with all this civil unrest and of course the election is on the horizon and one can reasonably expect a different outcome this time, and now there's Westy. 22 March Lyndon says he's going to move Westy up to Chief of Staff and it is the consensus of everybody that this is a kick upstairs but Lyndon denies this but you never, never know what's at the bottom of that man's mental puzzle. Anyway, this on the surface seems to open up new possibilities for pressing our campaign, in light of the absence from in-theater of an mentally intractable obstacle—or maybe—which is what I vaguely suspect—it is a feint to fend off Kennedy. On the twenty-second Lyndon releases word he intends to make a Viet Nam speech and he tells some guys to collect in the White House in the dining room to hash out a draft and give it to him when they're done.

You had Rusk, Humphrey, Clifford, Wheeler, Rostow, Christian, McPherson and they're all putting out inputs starting from somebody's initial draft that's quite hard, quite military—Lyndon's defending civilization etcetera—with just a titty bit on moving toward negotiations and Clifford tells them, like, that good sense and sound policy dictate that they've got to put the concentration on the negotiations aspect and keep in mind the Wisconsin primary on 2 April and that this is rather obviously the path of wisdom if Lyndon is to avoid the chance of a very damaging fiasco and he says I'm told that he begs to remind those present that the first principle of politics is political survival, which is to say job security, which apparently makes an impression, and they sit around the rest of the day considering what Hanoi is going to do if it gets a down rachet in air and what is going to happen if it doesn't move if it does and Humphrey says a partial cutback would look too political and Potato Face says something like he has no particular objection to a somewhat conciliatory tone in a speech but it is certain such a gesture will have no consequence in the conduct of the war due to Hanoi's obdurance and that it will be a good thing when this fact will be duly registered by all parties—banking as he is on Hanoi not talking unless the halt is a complete halt—and so after they've finished bandying things about they give their notes to McPherson to write a consensus draft and the essence being that McPherson writes in a halt north of the twentieth and complete halt if they cooperate, which is a very encouraging development indeed providing Lyndon doesn't cut his fingers off for writing such stuff when he shows it to him—apparently Lyndon doesn't say much of anything and he sends copies around without so much as a post-it on it, one to Freckle-Face Potato Head, who returns it with a notation that he has read it and hopes that the initiative will succeed although he deems it unlikely, and one to Bunker in Saigon—and at the same time you have—and here is a very, very significant triumph—Lyndon moves to get the troop albatross off his back and sends Wheeler out to meet with Westy in the Philippines on the twenty-fourth. He breaks it to him he's not getting the two hundred thousand in the time he put in for—the pressure is too heavy against it—and he's got to come down, and Westy ends up saying he'll settle for the two brigades—their permanent assignment—and thirteen, fourteen thousand support troops and he's thoroughly pissed.

He's squashed from being taken out of the show, he wanted to wrap this thing up into a nice tidy conclusion and get a fifth star and with this in his résumé go into politics, which makes you wonder, doesn't it? Here's a man with apparently an Eisenhower complex, obviously with a seriously defective appreciation of the magnitude of the differences between himself and an Eisenhower—and for that matter I think you might agree there are also a few differences between the wars, but, whatever, manifestly by his tractability the man is calculating that he is best not seen to be at odds in any way with the Commander-in-Chief—he's not about to pull a MacArthur—not a good move when he's looking to a political future life—and Bunker raises the whole bagful of his old objections to anything that can be—in his opinion—interpreted as a concession—his word is "indulgence."

But, he's a little bit less obstructionist—the word I would also use would be "objectionable"—less obstructionist and objectionable than usual since he doesn't think anything will come of it anyway, either, and so Lyndon is keeping his own counsel and with the reinforcements victory we allow ourselves to hope that now we can achieve a second, bigger victory considering the building political pressure but like I say you never know about Lyndon and you figure it would be a real nutcracker for him to be deflected from the warpath he's been on and you figure he's figuring if he deescalates it'll be tough to escalate up again and we don't have a report on him except one of our men sees him pacing up and down alone in the Oval Office calling Kennedy a bitch. And so then you have it's the twenty-fifth and you have Lyndon meets at the Department with his wise men, the obvious purpose for which is to have the approval again of the so-called experts, maybe his psyche requiring such approval because he recognizes in himself a weakness when it comes to geopolitics—world politics, war, things like that—so you have Lyndon and Clifford, Acheson, Taylor, Mathew Ridgeway, Henry Cabot Lodge, Douglas Dillon, Omar Bradley if you can imagine, Ball, Fortas, Mc-George Bundy, Arthur Dean, Goldberg, Cyrus Vance, John McCloy, Robert Murphy and first off they get some briefings on the current military picture, which are upbeat as usual but not all that upbeat at that and they start the discussion with distribution of the speech, which is apparently acceptable enough to the mavens: Fortas, Taylor and Murphy remain in the inflexible camp but do not present themselves as obstacles and Acheson, Bundy, Vance move somewhat toward the position of Ball and Goldberg, who are pushing for a complete halt, and

Lodge also kept to his usual stiff stance but without putting up any resistance, McCloy likewise, and Dean, Dillon, Bradley, Ridgeway expressed that there indeed needed to be some adjustment in the American position to get things off dead center and get things moving, and then they talked about the politics in the course of which Lyndon says he's not interested in this personal stuff, he's only interested in promoting the welfare of the American people, which sounds just a little bit pious to us who hear the speculation that he murdered his Senate opponent, and so things are looking quite good for our side but lo! spoken too soon because then on the twenty-eighth you have Potato Face and Rostow show Clifford and William Bundy and McPherson a revision that's all fire and piety—it highlights the ten thousand and omits the halt—and Clifford sees he's looking at about two tons of war rhetoric crap and says no, no this won't do, this won't go, it's the perfect target for all of Lyndon's enemies, the reaction would be very bad for him, it's got the wrong slant, all war, no peace, the politics of it would be impossible, the twentieth has to go back in, it implies greater budget deficits, with which the European bankers would be unhappy, and Potato and Rostow are intimidated and don't say anything other than to say it's well known how the generals feel about any kind of halt and everyone agrees that McPherson is to do a re-draft, and as it happens at the same time Lyndon is shopping the Potato-Rostow version with Mansfield and McCormack and some others and he got no buyers, and so McPherson worked all night and had a completed draft in the morning and I talked with him on the phone during the night and we discussed how we'd like it to go and I laid out some ideas and phrases which he took up and so don't let me brag but my input into this historic speech is not inconsiderable. McPherson tells me later this is the most important day of his life, 28 March '68, turning a critical speech which was hostile into an accommodating one, and he lays the draft before Lyndon and says this is the thinking of Clifford and the others and some time later Lyndon calls him and asks him to do some tinkering and from something he says for a horrible moment McPherson thinks he's gone back to Potato-Rostow and then to his enormous relief he realizes he hasn't, so here we are after a long and hard and bitter battle being within grasp of a major, major triumph—but we are very, very cautious: we don't know if Rostow might still pull something out of his bag of dirty tricks or if Lyndon might screw up the wording or set conditions, but we do know it's been a hard slog with Lyndon, like pushing a jackass through a swamp, so you have the speech goes through five more drafts and the cutback stays in and Katzenbach pushes for a halt above the nineteenth instead of the twentieth even though the brassies want to keep pounding Thanhhoa and Route Seven in between, and so here you have a big break for us.

Lyndon sends Potato off to a meeting of the allies in the Philippines so this makes Katzenbach Acting Secretary—the person at the helm in Washington, and you can tell Potato Head is fine with being far from where a halt that he figures for a disaster is being announced but on the other hand he always wants to be in the commander's seat, so what I do, I talk to Potato Face's wife, and I tell her I'm a little worried he's working awful hard and might be coming down with exhaustion and the warm weather of the Philippines might be just what the doctor ordered, which does the trick. Whatever else may eventuate, at least we won't have his face to have to look at for a few days. So taking advantage Katzenbach suggests restricting the bombing to close above the DMZ— the twentieth parallel is not something that's going to resonate with the people of Wisconsin—and he works out some wording for Lyndon; he's the guy that wrote that part about only bombing just north of the DMZ, where concentrations directly threaten American troops just south of the DMZ, thus sparing the part of the country where ninety percent of the people live—this is language Lyndon adopts only after asking Katzenbach to get Rostow's OK, so Katzenbach asks Rostow if he's OK with starting with keeping it close above the DMZ and Rostow says he has no opinion on that question since he believes any halt in any form is a grave mistake, so Katzenbach tells Lyndon he has Rostow's OK, and a couple of Lyndon's operatives—Horace Busby and Christian go over the speech on Sunday before the speech at nine—this is the thirty-first—and we're sweating whether an obstacle is going to be thrown up against us now when we're so close to our objective but it turns out we're fine and the only changes in the draft at this point are when Clifford asks Lyndon to tone down some phrases that aren't consistent with the otherwise peaceable noises he's making. And so then you have Lyndon invites Clifford and his wife for eight-thirty and they go upstairs with Ladybird and Valenti and Lyndon seems cheerful, which makes him wonder if Lyndon's about to pull a fast one, which probably wouldn't be good since when Lyndon pulls something out of his hat it's usually a turd, but he takes Clifford into the bedroom and springs it on him: he drops the N-bomb: he's not going to run, and he gives the speech, with the halt and with the with American boys fighting in foreign fields I'm not going to seek or accept nomination as your President peroration, as somebody calls it, and of course we never dreamed wild horses could drag Lyndon out of the White House but we study the shape of it and see that this seems maybe the least difficult way out for him and, whatever, we are damned glad he does it. Everything seems to have quieted down after a couple days but we are on our guard, trying to figure the odds he'll pull a Nasser and make the race anyway, which seems like a long shot but we're not putting down money because we know Lyndon is like an onion: sometimes you have to peel away a lot of garbage before you see what you've really got, and so what piece of genius do the Air Force generals pull but bomb Thanh Hoa on Wednesday and make their commander-in-chief a liar and cheat, as duly noted by the newspapers—not a smooth move with someone with Lyndon's temper, and a few careers were ended by the end of the day by that piece of idiocy—it does help if your enemies are idiots—and so then you have of course it goes without saying that Wheeler and Rostow and Potato Face and the other mothers are not about to give it up and keep at Lyndon but we're more than a match for them so when the VC had their little push in May and they wanted bombing up to at least the twentieth and to blast Thanh Hoa legally this time and Westy wants the B-52's over the base camps in Cambodia and ground troops in there we hold them off handily but then in June things get a good deal hairier for us when they lob a couple rockets into Saigon and Bunker twixes he wants payback—bombing on Hanoi—and the brassies are very, very itchy to go and telling Lyndon he really doesn't have any choice and the rockets keep coming and it seems we can't hang on much longer but then luckily the rockets stop and we're good, and so then you have Harriman and Vance make recommendations for a total halt—the end of July when you had a lull and they say they admit it's not deliberate but they recommend to Lyndon treating it like it was anyway and indicate to Hanoi now that they have deescalated—which I'm sure they'd be interested to learn—the bombing halt will stay as long as they don't escalate up again and Clifford is good with this and we get Humphrey and everybody else within range of those mutt's ears of his to talk it up with Lyndon and meanwhile Katzenbach and Bundy are in Paris talking to their opposites and the press there uncovers this proposal and Lyndon says he detects a pattern and folk are combining against him—it's a plot—which of course it is, and he expresses himself quite firmly against a total halt—a serious setback. So Harriman and Vance get to work to come up with something Lyndon will sign onto, the issue being that Lyndon always has to have guarantees—he won't sign an unconditional halt without a guarantee—and so Harriman and Vance come up with some pretty firm oral guarantees, which of course basically don't mean dink, and keep trying to sell Lyndon, telling him this is the most he can get, Hanoi will never go with anything in writing, this is pretty well near his last crack at getting movement with time going fast so they finally get Lyndon to bite, and so you have Bunker stirring it up with Thieu and Ky in Saigon.

He shoots off twixes that he is trying his best to bring them around but he moves to throw a monkey wrench into the process and tells Thieu he'll never have to sit down with the NLF: he knows he can't fend off the bombing halt with Lyndon on board but he can try to torpedo four-sided talks, so thanks to that man's good grace we spend a month with Thieu and Ky refusing to go to Paris, Thieu telling everybody he'll have nothing to do with a bombing halt and that morale in Saigon is going way down and the whole GVN might come down—of course he's working to stall everything off until Nixon gets in. Lyndon asks Nixon to give Thieu the word. Nixon doesn't want to do any favors but he sees he'll be in a bind if he gets locked in with Saigon and he delivers for Lyndon, whilst meanwhile Bunker is royally teed, much to our amusement. And all this time of course you have the brassies busting their buttons trying to get the bombing up and running again, feeding stuff to Lyndon and pointing to a couple hundred thousand NVA violations of the guarantees in the DMZ and their shelling of the cities and etcetera, telling him they could shorten it and save the lives of our boys and shit of the same gender.

But we keep in there close to Lyndon and we hold them off damn fine you have to admit and I guess what it is is you just have got to know how to go about doing stuff like this and then just go in there and do it and we just keep battling away and so we dood it. Yessir, we damn well did pull it off and so now you have these people claiming that us convincing Lyndon he couldn't continue on the path of catastrophe caused him to call it quits and so that we cost ourselves our jobs with Nixon getting in and all but I don't buy that because who really knows why he quit but if so, hey, what the fuck, you can't win at everything and I tell you it sure was something to win a really big one like that.

THIRTEEN

THE CORRESPONDENTS

In the morning Kramer was still drunk. He said having fucked his mood was excellent and amusing. He said he was in the mood to be amused. He and Friedman and I walked across the sidestreet to the Hotel Continental. Bataglia was reading the Daily News *and eating seaweed. Bataglia said he wondered when the race track would open again. He would have liked to attend the races at the race track. Friedman said we might go to Gia Dinh, where there was fighting. I said there was fighting by the Doi Canal bridge. Friedman said we might fly to Da Nang. Kramer said it was necessary for us to go to the journalists' briefing of the military command. The journalists' briefing of the military command was always amusing, he said. He wished to be amused. We rode on Cong Ly Street past the city limits to the airport.*

The military briefing officer stood stiffly before a map. Kramer winked and asked the officer if the war was going extremely well. The officer pointed to the map, explaining the ways in which the war was going well. Kramer said to Friedman he was pleasantly amused that the war had continued for seven years and was continuing to go well. He belched and asked the briefing officer if it was true that our side had a secret weapon with which we would completely defeat the enemy in two months. The briefing officer answered the question. The officer said there were a number of classified devices which would give the allies a substantial advantage in the fighting. Kramer asked if it was true that God was on our side.

He laughed drunkenly and vomited. A reporter of the Indianapolis Star *was angry about it.*

Bataglia said we could fly to Hong Kong for Buddha's birthday. We had quite a lot of fun that spring.

AT THE WAR

"At least they could stick a goddam light on the wall around here or something," said the fat man.

The fat man stood in the doorway leading onto the roof. There were the dim flashes of bombs exploding in the far distance. There was the rumbling sound of bombs exploding and the sound of rifles firing in the far distance. There was the sound of a police car in the distance.

The fat man carried two packs of beer. The fat man walked through the doorway onto the roof. In the dark the fat man stumbled over the threshold of the doorway and knocked into a chair and a table. The thumping sound of artillery rockets exploding in the nearer distance began.

"Damn it. I can't see diddle up here," said the fat man.

In the dark the fat man kicked a chair out of the way.

"Who's that sitting there?" said the fat man.

"Shoda," said the Japanese man.

"Shoda? The salesman?" said the fat man.

"Yes. I am a salesman," said the Japanese man.

"Stanley, you know. Third floor. RMK. You know, the construction company," said the fat man.

"Yes, I believe we have met, Mr. Stanley. Good evening," said the Japanese man.

"Hear that? One twenty-two rockets. Charlie's just beginning to bring those down from the north. They're Chinese. He's probably aiming for the new headquarters building where Westy has his office. That Wylie sitting there, right?" said the fat man.

"Small doubt about it," said the short man.

"You don't always got to be wise about what you say, Wylie," said the fat man.

There was the thumping sound of a salvo of bombs exploding in the far distance. The fat man moved a lounge chair and sat in it.

"What's happening now?" said the fat man.

"Nothing is happening, Mr. Stanley. They shoot a little and bomb far away," said the Japanese man.

"No big action? Just wait. There'll be action all right. Damn it all. Now ain't this a goddam shame. Some bastard broke a couple of the plastic strips on this chair. Somebody trying to make me sink right through the goddam thing," said the fat man.

Three jet airplanes flying in formation flew overhead. The faint sound of rifles firing in the far distance continued.

"Those are from the airport. See the way they're turning there. They're circling back to bomb near the airport. Did you see that in *Newsweek* with a picture of the MP's defending the embassy on the cover? They said they're supposed to be flying the shortest bombing missions in history, dumping the napalm right at the end of the runways. That ain't the way it is. They really have to take off and then circle back around to make the bombing runs near the airport," said the fat man.

The fat man's wife stood in the doorway leading onto the roof. The dim flashes and rumbling sounds of bombs exploding in the far distance continued.

"Are you up here yet, George?" said the fat man's wife.

"Over here, doll. What's the matter, you blind?" said the fat man.

"I keep a pretty good eye on you," said the fat man's wife. The fat man's wife sat in a chair.

"Hand me a can of beer, George. Haven't you asked these two gentlemen if they want a can of beer?" said the fat man's wife.

"Well, not yet I haven't. I didn't think they wanted any," said the fat man.

The fat man offered the Japanese man and the short man a can of beer. The fat man handed a can of beer to his wife, the short man and the Japanese man. The fat man drank from a can of beer.

"Damn it all. You left the refrigerator door open again, didn't you, doll? I know you did. This stuff feels warm," said the fat man.

"No I didn't," said the fat man's wife.

"Give me a cookie, doll," said the fat man.

"I don't have any cookies. I didn't bring any cookies up with me. You said you were bringing a bag of Hydrox with you," said the fat man's wife.

"Oh for Christ sake, what's wrong with you? You were supposed to bring up the goddam bag of cookies, you said you were going to. Go on, go and get the goddam cookies for us," said the fat man.

There were brighter flashes and louder thumping sounds of bombs exploding at a nearer distance. The fat man's wife stood up and walked through the door.

"They almost dropped a load of napalm practically on top of my head once. It was up near Nha Trang, We were putting in a little road one morning. A can of napalm accidentally comes loose off of the airplane and lands maybe three hundred yards away. You should see the wind that stuff makes. You can't breathe, either, because the fire uses up all the air. The Cong didn't get far at Nha Trang last month," said the fat man.

The thin man and the thin man's wife came through the door onto the roof. They carried paper cups filled with soft drink.

"How do you do?" said the Japanese man.

"Quite well," said the thin man.

"Good. How are you?" said the thin man's wife.

"There ain't nothing much to see up here, Franks. You come up here tomorrow if you want to see something," said the fat man.

"The name's Franklin," said the thin man.

"It's pretty up here in the evening, isn't it, even though it's scary? Are there many mosquitoes out tonight? If it's anything like it was last time up here, I'm going back down," said the thin man's wife.

The thin man and the thin man's wife sat in chairs. There was the loud thumping sound of a large bomb exploding in the distance.

"Dear me. What was that? It sounds like someone blew something up. I'll never forget going by the ruins of the shop that blew up with all those people in it," said the thin man's wife.

"I imagine that was a bomb from an airplane, dear," said the thin man.

"You are correct: a five-hundred pounder. The biggest they use except in the fifty-twos. They use seven-fifty and thousand pounders in the B-52's," said the fat man.

"You did lock the door of our room when we came up, didn't you, Howard? The people who work at the hotel could still get in and steal something, I suppose. I wouldn't really blame them, they're so poor," said the thin man's wife.

"Did you see that? There. That white streak way off there beyond the lights of the docks. Probably a spotter rocket from a spotter plane showing the bombers where to hit. I got real good eyes for seeing little things like that. I got twenty-ten vision. You know the way to see something real dim? Look at it a little bit out of the corner of your eye," said the fat man.

"Oh dear. Have I lost my string of green beads again, Howard? Did you hear them drop? Do you remember if I wore them at dinner? Maybe they just fell off now," said the thin man's wife.

The thin man lit a cigarette lighter and looked around on the roof. "I don't remember. I don't see them," said the thin man.

The fat man lit a cigarette. There was the sound of a jeep speeding through the street below. In the street three Vietnamese policemen shouted and laughed.

"Would you give me a cigarette, Howard? Do you think it's safe to smoke here tonight? Maybe someone will shoot at us if they see the light of the cigarettes," said the thin man's wife.

"I don't think so. There ain't many Cong in this neighborhood. But you know why I say they wouldn't? The VC couldn't see the light of a cigarette. You know why not? They got bad vision on account of not eating the right vegetables. Besides, you see the way I hold my cigarette, with the lighted end cupped in my hand? That's a habit I picked up in the army when you learn to smoke that way in case the enemy soldiers could be observing," said the fat man.

"So you were in the army, were you? I suppose you had a great deal of experience fighting in Korea, too," said the thin man.

"Well, no, Franklin, in fact I didn't get to see Korea. I was a little early for that one. I was in the army just before Korea. But I'll tell you what—I was in the middle of a riot in Jersey City in the army once just like Detroit last year. I don't know whether you know it or not, Franklin, but it's a fact there ain't any kind of combat that's hairier than a riot," said the fat man.

"It must be awful to be in the middle of a riot," said the thin man's wife.

"Where was it you saw combat, Franklin?" said the fat man.

"I wasn't in the army," said the thin man.

"I thought everybody that was half normal got in the army," said the fat man.

The fat man smoked a cigarette. The fat man drank from a can of beer. The sound of bombs exploding in the far distance continued.

"The second wave hits tonight," said the fat man.

"I don't think so. Not in the middle of the week," said the thin man.

"I said tonight. It's exactly one day less than a month after the Tet new year's day on the thirtieth of January. That's the way the Cong works, launching offensives at the odd times to throw everybody off," said the fat man.

"I see. Ordinarily you would expect them to attack exactly a month later," said the thin man.

"It's tonight all right. They're going to move in on the city with a few of those new Russian light tanks they took Lang Vei with. Our maid on the third floor has a brother in the police department. He has all the stuff on it," said the fat man.

"They'll use M-48 tanks they bought surplus at the Kaufman Army Navy Store on Forty-Second Street in Manhattan," said the short man.

"Surplus? What are you talking about? Wylie, are you trying to be funny? If you'd cut that out once in a while, you wouldn't sound so dumb all the time. Let them use whatever they feel like. If we don't beat them regardless there's something wrong somewhere, believe me," said the fat man.

"Certainly it is very nice weather we are having, do you believe?" said the Japanese man.

"Tomorrow it rains," said the fat man.

"Why do you believe that, Mr. Stanley? I believe the *Post* writes it will be fair weather tomorrow," said the Japanese man.

"Did you see the clouds over there before sunset. They were cumulus clouds. Any time you see cumulus clouds in the west in this city before sunset it rains the next day. A guy in the Air Force weather department at Tan Son Nhut told me that. You keep track. I never known it to fail once," said the fat man.

The fat man drank from a can of beer.

"That's not the west. That's the northwest. Those lights are the airport runway," said the thin man.

"Howard, don't talk that way," said the thin man's wife.

"That's west, Franklin, maybe a little north. Mainly it's west. You'd best wear your raincoat tomorrow if you don't want to get wet," said the fat man.

"Do the Viet Cong attack when it rains?" said the thin man.

"Honey, don't say anything to Mr. Stanley unless you can say it nicely," said the thin man's wife.

"As a matter of fact, Franklin, you're right—they do attack in the rain. You seen those black shorts they wear, haven't you? They wear those especially for walking through the rice paddies and for wet weather. They can run faster because they're not wearing much," said the fat man.

"I thought everyone said the Viet Cong wear black pajamas. I guess you're talking about short pajamas," said the thin man.

"I'm talking about black short pants, Franklin. Those black uniforms are only pajamas when they sleep in them at night if they do. If it rains tonight, they attack for sure. After midnight, you know. They always attack after midnight. Charlie always hits between three and four in the morning," said the fat man.

"Maybe the Viet Cong would win the war if they went naked," said the short man.

There was the sound of a loudspeaker truck passing in the street below. The fat man's wife stood in the doorway leading onto the roof. She carried a bag of cookies.

"Are you still up here, George?" said the fat man's wife.

"Where you think I'd go, smarts? Jump five stories to the sidewalk?" said the fat man.

"I thought you ascended to heaven to get your reward for always talking politely," said the fat man's wife.

"Give me a cookie," said the fat man.

The fat man's wife sat in a chair. There was the loud thumping sound of several bombs exploding simultaneously in the distance. The fat man's wife held out the bag of cookies to the fat man. The fat man took three cookies from the bag.

"Oh, why didn't you say the Franklins are here? I hope you've offered them some beer, dear," said the fat man's wife.

"Use you eyes, why don't you, doll? They already got something to drink," said the fat man.

"Did you get those from the machine on the second floor? I'm glad they finally got somebody to fix that machine. I didn't think they ever would.

"Oh my. That bomb sounded like it was awfully near. They're not dropping any bombs very near here, are they, Howard?" said the thin man's wife.

The fat man's wife held out the bag of cookies to the thin man's wife.

"God damn, doll. Don't give all the cookies away. There ain't a carload of them there, you know. Give me a piece of the spearmint," said the fat man.

"Have you been drinking the beer in my can? I bet you have, haven't you? I took all the chewing gum from my purse and put it on the chiffonier. I don't have it with me," said the fat man's wife.

"Jesus Christ. Can't you do anything right? Go down and get it then," said the fat man.

"No. You'll have to go get that yourself if you want it. You can't chew gum while you're eating cookies, anyway," said the fat man's wife.

"Go and get the goddam chewing gum, doll," said the fat man.

"No. You heard what I said, George," said the fat man's wife.

The fat man drank from a can of beer. The sound of bombs exploding continued.

"Jesus Christ," said the fat man.

"It's really terrible not to be able to go anywhere at night like this. I think everybody's getting a little nervous having to stay indoors at night all the time. I wonder if they couldn't show movies in the restaurant downstairs or something," said the thin man's wife.

The fat man drank from a can of beer. There was the sound of two airplanes flying over the city. Many brilliant white flares slowly descended over the city.

"Oh look at those. They're kind of pretty, aren't they?" said the thin man's wife.

"Those are illumination flares again, dear," said the thin man.

"You know what kind of airplanes are dropping those flares now, Franklin?" said the fat man.

"No, I don't," said the thin man.

"I didn't think you did. C-47's. The airplanes with all the Gatling guns on them," said the fat man.

The fat man drank from a can of beer. The sound of bombs exploding in the distance became fainter. The thin man's wife stepped to the edge of the roof and looked over the edge.

"Look. It almost seems as light as day out with those burning. Goodness, aren't those things bright? What are they made of that make them so bright?" said the thin man's wife.

"Flares are made out of white phosphorous. They have little parachutes on them. That's what makes them come down so slow," said the fat man.

"Why does it take them so long to burn up?" said the thin man's wife.

The fat man drank from a can of beer. There was the sound of a machine-gun firing in the far distance. The thin man's wife crouched low on the roof and then stood up.

I guess that shooting wasn't near here after all," said the thin man's wife.

"Well, tell her the answer to her question," said the fat man's wife.

"You got to say something, huh, dearie? Well, there ain't no answer to the question. It just takes them that long to burn, that's all," said the fat man.

"Oh look there. Oh my. There are two little boys down there. They're stealing things from the cars parked along the street. Howard, our car isn't parked on that street in front, is it? They'd better stop that or they'll be shot, won't they, if the police see them? That's what the police are supposed to do, isn't it, Howard, shoot anybody on the street no matter who he is?" said the thin man's wife.

"That's right," said the fat man.

"Yes. That's right. I don't imagine they would shoot at little boys, though," said the thin man.

"This is such a poor country, isn't it, Howard? I wonder if you're really doing the people here much good with all the aid we're giving them. There are so many people hare living in slums and dirty clothes. I just wonder sometimes if the people in this country really want as to be here. Sometimes I think maybe it would be better if we just left and let the communists run the government," said the thin man's wife.

"Well, we're here, anyway," said the thin man.

"Johnson says we could leave this place in six months. I happen to know for a fact that we decide to get out of this place tomorrow, it takes us at least a year to get out. Longer if they want to take out all the heavy stuff they brought in," said the fat man,

"Oh, oh. That little boy just broke the window of that car. He shouldn't do that. I hope he didn't cut his hand," said the thin man's wife.

"I been out on the streets two or three times after seven o'clock in the last couple of weeks. One time two of these South Vietnamese policemen just did see me before I ducked behind this car. I was a little scared, I'll admit to you. I really thought I was a goner. You know what, those two policemen didn't pay any goddam attention to me. None of those South Vietnamese give a damn, you know. All of them are in it only for what they can get out of it," said the fat man.

"Oh, I don't think that's true at all. I've met a lot of very nice Vietnamese people while we've been here. They all have such good manners," said the thin man's wife.

"President Thieu's the one that thought up this curfew bit. He wasn't thinking of the Cong raiding at night so much, he's got his own reason. I bet none of you guys know why," said the fat man.

"To keep his wife off the streets," said the short man.

"Shut up, Wylie. Thieu is after Vice President Ky. The way it is, Ky wants to knock over Thieu so naturally Thieu is looking for a way to come down hard on Ky. So what Thieu does, he declares this curfew so no one can be on the street at night.

"You see Ky owns the Tropicana nightclub and Thieu thinks it can't do any business if he puts on a curfew. But it doesn't work out that way since the people going to the nightclub figure out ways of getting there anyway, so Thieu orders all the nightclubs in the country closed down like he did last week.

"It's all on account of Ky. When the Tet offensive first started, some people figured it for a coup by Ky. That Ky would take over the government in a minute if he had half the chance. You know he didn't like it much when Thieu pushed him out of running for the presidency before the elections. That's the real stuff on the curfew," said the fat man.

The fat man drank from a can of beer. The sound of bombs exploding in the distance became louder and became fainter. The thin man's wife sat in a chair.

"I think President Thieu is doing the best he can under the terrible conditions he has to work under. Howard and I saw him from not far away one day at a reception at the Independence Palace and he talked and I think he gave a very good speech. He has such an open, honest face and I know he means well. I wish he would get his teeth fixed, though, they're terrible looking.

"I've never actually seen Vice President Ky but I can't trust him as much as I trust President Thieu. He looks kind of tricky and I've seen pictures of him wearing a silly purple uniform and a yellow scarf. I don't think a man should dress like that if he wants to be one of the leaders of his country," said the thin man's wife.

"That's what's wrong with this messed-up country. It's not organized right. What do they do with that dummy Rossi in my section today? What else? They take him and promote him to supervisor. Rossi! That jerk don't know peas about beans. You should of seen him botch up the barracks we were putting up out at Bien Hoa a few months back. I never seen anybody so dumb. And I been a lousy foreman in that section three months before Rossi even showed up out here. It was me who figured everything out and did all the work ever since, too.

"That's why we're not winning this war today, because they put jerks like that Rossi in positions of responsibility. You say you saw Thieu from a distance. Well, I shook hands with him once. He's not a bad guy," said the fat man.

A flare descended in the distance. A jet airplane flew overhead.

"That was an F-100," said the fat man.

"It was a Phantom," said the thin man.

"Not hardly, my boy. It was an F-100. I can tell an F-100 a mile off," said the fat man.

"Well, that wasn't an F-100. It was a Phantom. Twin fan-tails. The Phantom whine," said the thin man.

"You're crazy, Franklin. There ain't never been a Phantom jet made yet that made a noise like that. If you don't know that, you don't know a goddam thing about what you're talking about," said the fat man.

"I think not," said the thin man.

"Can it, will you? Just what do you know? When you ever been up in one of those jets? I been up in an F-100 three times. A pal of mine in Illinois took me up in an F-100 three times. You don't think I know what an F-100 sounds like," said the fat man.

"When did you ever go up in a jet?" said the fat man's wife.

"Will you be quiet? I said I went up in a jet. When doesn't make any difference what a jet sounds like," said the fat man.

The sound of a machine-gun firing nearby began. Glowing green tracer bullets began to rise intermittently from between nearby buildings and descend in long arcs.

The fat man, the fat man's wife, the thin man, the short man and the Japanese man ducked their heads. The thin man's wife crouched low on the roof of the building.

"My goodness. Howard, are you all right? Are they shooting at us? That was awfully close, wasn't it?" said the thin man's wife.

"It's two or three blocks away," said the thin man.

"You don't suppose they'd shoot at us, do you?" said the thin man's wife.

"I known cases where the gooks shot nuns through the head point blank," said the fat man.

"And we all know about a similar case involving idiot General Loan, don't we? Except that he shot a handcuffed man through the head for the benefit of the photographers," said the short man.

"I wasn't far from that street when he did that. I think I heard the shot," said the fat man.

"I think we ought to go downstairs now, Howard," said the thin man's wife.

"There's no need to go downstairs, dear. That gunfire isn't coming anywhere near here. It's probably a soldier or two shooting at a rooftop somewhere where they thought they saw a sniper," said the thin man.

The fat man drank from a can of beer. There was the sound of a bomb exploding nearby.

"Hah! You hear that? That shows how much you know about it, Franklin. Of course I realize you're a clerk, Franklin, and you sit behind a desk all day so I don't expect you to be too familiar with the way Charlie works. Those aren't snipers they're shooting at. Those are bombers. That was a claymore mine you just heard go off, a booby trap. Some poor slob just stepped on the trip wire. The VC fasten claymore mines to the lampposts," said the fat man.

"If the Viet Cong plant bombs and walk away, who are they shooting at? Tell us that," said the fat man's wife.

"Let's be a little accurate here, guy. I don't happen to be a clerk. The fact is I'm the manager of one of the most important offices in-theater," said the thin man.

The fat man drank from a can of beer. There was the sound of a short burst of machine-gun fire.

"Who said they got away, stupid? They haven't got away. They surprised them trying to plant the bombs. Then there's a firefight while they kill them trying to get away. It happens every day," said the fat man.

The very tall man stood in the doorway leading onto the roof. There was the sound of jet airplanes flying in the far distance. There was the sound of artillery guns firing in the distance. The very tall man smoked a cigar.

"You here, George boy?" said the very tall man.

"Who's that? Hal? Here," said the fat man.

"My dear boy, how can you waste all your time up here? Who else is here? Evening to you all," said the very tall man.

"Evening," said the Japanese man.

"I'm Franklin. My wife. George's wife is here, and Mr. Wylie," said the thin man.

"I should say it's nice to see you but I can't see you so I can't say that, right?" said the very tall man.

"Give Hal a can of beer, George," said the fat man's wife.

"What? Beer? You joke. I never touch the stuff. Except in emergencies. George, I come to take you away from this pedestrian drinking of beer. Come on to Frank's. At least we can indulge in a few decent stingers. Still, as it's gratis, I'll take it," said the very tall man.

The fat man handed the very tall man a can of beer. The very tall man went to the edge of the roof and stood with a hand on his hip. There was the sound of bombs and artillery shells exploding in the far distance. The very tall man stood looking at the city of Saigon and into the distance beyond it.

"Well, who's winning?" said the very tall man.

"I think you should be a little careful that close to the edge of the roof, Mr. Brewster. There was just some shooting that didn't seem to be very far away," said the thin man's wife.

"Maybe there ain't no action now, but there will be at three o'clock tomorrow morning," said the fat man.

"This beer isn't bad. Come on, Georgie, let's make it to Frank's. I think it closes at eleven. They got a special today, bloody Marys for sixty cents. Come on. Bring your wife along," said the very tall man.

"I don't think I want to make Frank's tonight, Hal," said the fat man.

"Oh look over there. That looks like a Vietnamese man on the roof of that building over there, doesn't it? You don't suppose he's a communist with a gun, do you?" said the thin man's wife.

"You know a good way to win this war, folks? Charge all the Viet Cong union dues. The Viet Cong are organized like one big tight union, correct? Well, all you have to do is charge them outrageous dues like they do in our union and they couldn't afford to pay them and so they'd complain and quit the organization. You know what they're thinking about doing to us now, George? Raising the dues another three dollars a month. I'd make more money in this country as a Montagnard mercenary," said the very tall man.

"Howard has never had to belong to a union," said the thin man's wife.

"He will when they get around to organizing clerks," said the fat man.

"Did Hotchkiss pay you the twenty dollars he owed you? He owes me thirty-five," said the very tall man.

"He paid me," said the fat man.

"George, I was supposed to get that twenty dollars for draperies, remember?" said the fat man's wife.

"Time's a-wasting, Georgie. You know, it's unhealthy for you to stay up here so long in this dark. You'll wear out your visual purple," said the very tall man.

"I really don't think I feel like it, Hal. Anyway, I think Frank said he was closing up at night because there weren't so many people beating the curfew. There a lot of police in the street now?" said the fat man.

"No, no, George boy. Would I ever ask you to do anything dangerous? Well, not tonight, anyway, pal. I got an MP sergeant friend of mine downstairs waiting for us. There'll be no trouble about the curfew. We all go down the street to Frank's with a military escort.

"You should have seen your husband move out last Saturday, Mrs. Stanley, when we sneaked over to Frank's after curfew. I bet you didn't know old George could run that fast. Old George thought the police were just around the corner," said the very tall man.

"The police *were* just around the corner. You wouldn't be laughing here here today if you hadn't of hustled too," said the fat man.

"Even the Queen Mary used to make twenty knots," said the short man.

"Shut up Wylie. If anybody wants any of your lip, they'll ask for it," said the fat man.

"I guess I could use a couple drinks, Hal," said the fat man.

"No, George," said the fat man's wife.

"What?" said the fat man.

"You're not going to go to any bars tonight. You've drunk too much beer. You'd get sick again if you drank anything else," said the fat man's wife.

"All right. If you don't want to go, I'll go with Hal by myself," said the fat man.

"No you won't. You're not going to get drunk and sick tonight," said the fat man's wife.

The fat man stood up.

"I'm going with Hal. Maybe I'll just drink beer," said the fat man.

"Another time, then, Georgie. That's what you get sitting in the dark drinking this nasty stuff. Maybe tomorrow. You still owe me a shot, don't you?" said the very tall man.

"I'll go with you, Hal" said the fat man.

"No you won't," said the fat man's wife.

"Chin up, Georgie. The war can't go on forever. Thanks for the beer. Good night," said the very tall man.

The very tall man walked through the doorway. The fat man lay down in the lounge chair. The fat man drank from a can of beer.

"You know something, doll? I don't like it when you act like that," said the fat man.

"I can't help that," said the fat man's wife.

The fat man drank from a can of beer. There was the sound of a tank moving through a street in the distance.

"God damn. This jackass chair is pinching me," said the fat man.

"It wouldn't pinch you if you'd lie in it straight," said the fat man's wife.

"Will you just keep it quiet, doll? It so happens this goddam thing is busted. Three of these strip things here are busted. I know it wasn't this way yesterday. That bugs me to hell," said the fat man.

"Sabotage, no doubt," said the short man.

"Franklin, let me have your chair. That's the chair I usually sit in up here," said the fat man.

"I'd rather not. I kind of like this chair," said the thin man.

"Now, honey, be polite," said the thin man's wife.

"Come on, get up. You're so goddam skinny you can just lie on the part of this that ain't busted," said the fat man.

"You could lie on that part of it too if you would go on a diet," said the fat man's wife.

"You're asking for it, aren't you, dearie? Give me that chair now, Franklin," said the fat man.

"I think I prefer the chair I'm sitting in to that one," said the thin man.

"Get up, Franklin," said the fat man.

"For heaven's sake, honey, let Mr. Stanley sit in the chair if he likes that one better," said the thin man's wife.

"I don't think that is necessary at all. There are other chairs on the roof of this building," said the thin man.

"Stand up, Franklin. Or maybe you want me to help you stand up?" said the fat man.

The fat man stood up.

"Calm down, George," said the fat man's wife.

"Since when has a person been required to surrender his chair whenever another person likes it better than the one he's sitting in?" said the thin man.

"Franklin, I don't like your attitude. Stand up or I'll make you stand up," said the fat man.

"George, get down off your hind legs," said the fat man's wife.

"I told you to shut up, dearie. I'm waiting, Franklin. Give me that chair or I'm taking you on right now."

"He's going to take him on. Oh my. Remember now, boys, there'll be no kicking, scratching, hair-pulling or crying. The winner is king of the block and the loser will buy sundae treats for everyone," said the short man.

"That's exactly right. Both of you men are acting just like little children. Both of you stop this silliness right now," said the thin man's wife.

"George, sit down," said the fat man's wife.

"I believe there is a similar chair next to mine that is empty, Mr. Stanley, if you wish," said the Japanese man.

"George, sit down," said the fat man's wife.

"Well, I don't know. Maybe I will. All right, I will. Franklin, you're lucky. I'll let you off this time. But that doesn't give you a license to keep on acting like a bastard," said the fat man.

The fat man stepped to a chair. He moved the chair and sat in it. The fat man drank from a can of beer.

"George, give the Franklins some beer. And give these men another can of beer, too," said the fat man's wife.

"There ain't enough here," said the fat man.

"George," said the fat man's wife.

The fat man handed a can of beer to the Japanese man, the short man, the thin man and the thin man's wife. The fat man drank from a can of beer. Seven helicopters flying in close formation flew overhead. There were blinking red, green and white dome lights on the helicopters.

"I wonder where the soldiers in those are going. I hope they don't have to go where all that shooting was coming from. I'm sure they'd all be killed if they tried to get off those airplanes where they were shooting," said the thin man's wife.

"I bet Franklin doesn't even know those helicopters don't always carry passengers. Those are Hueys. They fly them sometimes with just a couple of machine-gunners at the doors. I bet Franklin never even seen any of those new armed helicopters they got now, the Cobras. I seen those working quite a few times. I saw one tearing up a piece of Cholon the other day. They'll blow up all of Saigon with those birds," said the fat man.

"I can do without your comments, Stanley," said the thin man.

"Oh, I don't think you should talk about blowing up the city at all. Think what would happen to all the people living in it," said the thin man's wife.

The fat man drank from a can of beer. There was the sound of a pistol firing once in the distance. The whistle of an ambulance passing in a street nearby began.

"Oh my. That's an ambulance, isn't it, Howard? I remember the ambulance had a whistle that came when that poor old white-haired gentleman fell over and died in the lobby. He was such a nice old man. He told us all about all the adventures he had importing things from these countries. There's the ambulance there.

"Howard, don't you suppose we should go to the hospital again even though they sent Dottie's nephew back to the United States? It felt so good to help cheer up the other wounded soldiers in the hospital. Those nurses work so hard, they ought to be paid twice as much as they are. It certainly makes you think when you see all those soldiers with the horrible wounds in them," said the thin man's wife.

"I seen a truck driver once that was wounded down by My Tho on the highway. His truck hits a mine and blows sky high, then I seen this guy he was lying there screaming in the road next to what's left of the truck. His leg was blown clean off. The leg is lying right there beside him on the road. They put a tourniquet on him but he screams he won't let them move him unless they take the leg along with him. I don't know he thinks they can sew it back on or what. Believe me, they never could of sewed that leg back on. It was all busted up," said the fat man.

"Oh, how horrible," said the thin man's wife.

"I could tell you about plenty more bad things I seen if I wanted to," said the fat man.

The fat man drank from a can of beer.

"Now the sky'll start clouding up. Then nobody sees anything with those flares until after they drop through the clouds so our air ain't no use. The VC'll open up. You notice the VC always got cover whenever they hit. They always got camouflage, too, old Charlie does. My guess is this time they show up dressed like Arvins. They'll wear a red handkerchief around their arm like those commandoes that tried to get into the embassy at Tet," said the fat man.

"Certainly now it is a very beautiful night," said the Japanese man.

"You see that bright star up there in line with that green light there? That's the north pole."

"I guess you mean the North Star," said the thin man.

"All right, Franklin, North Star. It's the North Pole Star, the same thing," said the fat man,

"My, there are a lot of stars out tonight, aren't there?" said the thin man's wife.

"That's the Big Dipper. That's Cassiopeia. That's the Little Dipper with the North Star in it. I know all those constellations, I learned them all one time for the hell of it. Over there's Ursa Major and over there's Ursa Minor," said the fat man.

"That is not Ursa Minor," said the thin man.

"Howard, I asked you," said the thin man's wife.

"It couldn't be Ursa Minor," said the thin man.

"That's Ursa Minor," said the fat man.

"Certainly all the stars tonight in the sky are very beautiful," said the Japanese man.

"You said the Little Dipper is over there, Stanley. Well, the Little Dipper is the same constellation as Ursa Minor," said the thin man.

"It doesn't make any difference, honey. Please let's not argue about it," said the thin man's wife.

The fat man drank from a can of beer.

"Let me tell you something, Franklin. You're nuts. Some day you're going to open your mouth and know what you're talking about, but not any time soon. The Little Dipper is the Little Dipper and Ursa Minor is Ursa Minor," said the fat man.

"They are both the same thing," said the thin man.

"Howard," said the thin man's wife.

"Here we go again," said the short man.

The fat man drank from a can of beer.

"You know something, Franklin? You couldn't fill a fucking tooth with what you know about the stars," said the fat man.

"Don't swear like that, George," said the fat man's wife.

"Excuse me, I believe Mr. Franklin is correct in what he said about the Little Dipper. I believe they teach at the university that the Little Dipper is known also by the name of Ursa Minor," said the Japanese man.

"Now just wait, Stanley. Just watch what you're saying to me," said the thin man.

The fat man drank from a can of beer.

"Franklin, you've been letting your fucking mouth overload your fucking brain," said the fat man.

"George, I said don't swear like that," said the fat man's wife.

"Stanley, shut your mouth," said the thin man.

The fat man stood up.

"All right. Make me, Franklin. Try and make me shut up," said the fat man.

"Oh for God's sake, George," said the fat man's wife.

The thin man stood up.

"You're not talking to me that way," said the thin man.

"Buddy, I'll talk to you any goddam way I feel like talking to you," said the fat man.

"My. We have two real tigers here, don't we?" said the short man.

"Stop it, honey. I want to go downstairs now," said the thin man's wife.

"Go on and try something, bigmouth. I'll push that flapping face of yours in," said the fat man.

"George, sit down," said the fat man's wife.

"Stanley, don't talk to me that way again," said the thin man.

"Come on. Go ahead. Try something. I'm waiting. You're not getting out of it this time, Franklin," said the fat man.

"Wait a second, you two. How about letting me stand holding up my lighter over your heads so at least you can see to hit each other. I'll pretend I'm the Statue of Liberty," said the short man.

"George, you will sit down and be quiet now," said the fat man's wife.

"Hah! I see you ain't moving, Franklin. You're thinking you'd better not try anything rough if you don't want your head smashed in, is that it?" said the fat man.

"George," said the fat man's wife.

"This sure is exciting," said the short man.

"George," said the fat man's wife.

"Well, Franklin," said the fat man.

"George," said the fat man's wife.

"Well, all right. If that's the way you feel about it, doll. Maybe this is not place to fight, anyway. You're damn lucky you didn't make a move, Franklin. I would of killed you. I tell you what, Franklin. There's a gym downstairs. Tomorrow at five thirty after I knock off work I'll be down in the gym waiting for you. They got gloves down there and I'll settle with you fair and square. Maybe you'll show up there if you're not chicken to," said the fat man.

The fat man sat down. The fat man drank from a can of beer.

"I agree to that," said the thin man.

"Honey," said the thin man's wife.

The thin man sat down.

"They've got fencing swords down there too," said the short man.

"What are you thinking of, George? You don't know how to box," said the fat man's wife.

"Shut up, doll," said the fat man.

"Really, honey. This is all so silly. Mr. Stanley didn't really mean anything bad by what he said. Tell Mr. Stanley you apologize and make it up, darling," said the thin man's wife.

"I meant what I said," said the fat man.

"Be quiet, George. Watch the airplanes go by. Those are airplanes over there, aren't they? Are those bombs they're dropping I hear?" said the fat man's wife.

"One-oh-five's," said the fat man.

"What's that?" said the fat man's wife.

"Artillery, idiot," said the fat man.

"I really think you should apologize now for what you said to Mr. Stanley, sweetheart," said the thin man's wife.

"I think not," said the thin man.

"Honey," said the thin man's wife.

The dim flashes and rumbling sounds of bombs exploding in the far distant continued. The fat man drank from a can of beer.

"The hell with this. I'm getting out of here. There ain't nothing to see up here. Come on, doll. Let's go downstairs," said the fat man.

The fat man stood up.

"It's so stuffy in the rooms downstairs. It's too cold to turn on the air conditioner. I froze when I tried that the other day," said the fat man's wife.

"What's on TV now?" said the fat man.

" 'Combat' is on at ten-thirty. They only use the old wars on that, though. They never show anything about the Viet Nam War on 'Combat,' " said the short man.

"Knock it off, Wylie," said the fat man.

"George, calm down," said the fat man's wife.

"They showed a program with Bob Hope in Viet Nam. I don't know why they can't show the hero of 'Combat' in Viet Nam," said the short man.

"Tomorrow at five thirty, Franklin," said the fat man.

"Are you really going to try to box him, dear?" said the fat man's wife.

"I'll be there," said the thin man.

"I suppose the exercise might do you some good," said the fat man's wife.

"Now you two men just shake hands and make up. You're both acting just like little spoiled brats," said the thin man's wife.

"And I'll take this while I'm at it," said the fat man.

The fat man took the can of beer the thin man had been drinking from.

"Oh good God, George, give Mr. Franklin's beer back," said the fat man's wife.

"Why should I buy beer for a bigmouth?" said the fat man.

"Really, I have to apologize for the way my husband has been acting," said the fat man's wife.

"Don't talk to them, doll. Come on," said the fat man.

"Don't pull at me, George," said the fat man's wife.

"Honey, please say good night to the Stanleys," said the thin man's wife.

"Good night, Mrs. Stanley," said the thin man.

"Howard. Good night, Mr. and Mrs. Stanley. It was really very, very nice seeing you here again. I know you men will forget all about this silly talk about fighting," said the thin man's wife.

"Good evening to you, Mr. and Mrs. Stanley," said the Japanese man.

"Good night, everyone," said the fat man's wife.

"We might advertise the big fight. You might charge admission and I might make book. Good night," said the short man.

The fat man and the fat man's wife walked towards the doorway. In the dark the fat man collided with a chair.

"Are you blind?" said the fat man's wife.

"Just shut your trap," said the fat man.

The fat man and the fat man's wife walked through the doorway.

"Darling, you're not going to be silly, are you? You're not really going to go to the gymnasium tomorrow and try to fight with that big heavy man, are you?" said the thin man's wife.

"He won't show up, anyway. He was just a little drunk tonight," said the thin man.

"If a big heavy man like that were to hit you, darling, I'm sure he could injure you very severely. You won't try to fight him, will you? There's no reason at all for you and Mr. Stanley to fight," said the thin man's wife.

"That big tub of fat injure me? You can't be serious. What do you want me to do, let that idiot know-it-all say anything he likes to me?" said the thin man.

"Honey, I know Mr. Stanley is a little annoying that way but he does know a lot about the war here and he's really a very nice person," said the thin man's wife.

"He can't talk to me the way he did," said the thin man.

"I don't want you to fight anyone, dear. There's simply no point in two sensible grown men like you and Mr. Stanley fighting with each other for no reason. Promise me you won't fight with him," said the thin man's wife.

"I won't have to fight anyone. He won't show up at the gym. I may not show up there, either," said the thin man.

The loud sound of rifles firing nearby began. The Japanese man and the thin man ducked down. The thin man's wife crouched low on the roof. The thin man walked cautiously to the edge of the roof and looked over it.

"Goodness. What's that, Howard? I'm sure they're fighting right on the next block. Howard, I wish you wouldn't stand so close to the edge of the roof when they're shooting like that," said the thin man's wife.

"They're not shooting on the next block. It's three or four blocks away, at least," said the thin man.

"Oh dear. I hope they're not shooting at the army policemen again with the black helmets. That poor boy we saw that day that was covered up in the street, Howard, he was a policeman, wasn't he? That was his black helmet with a bullet hole through it they showed us, wasn't it? Think of that poor boy's mother when they tell her. This war is so awful. I wish they would stop it," said the thin man's wife.

"They may be shooting at the MPs. Snipers have been shooting at the MP jeeps," said the thin man.

"I just wonder if we should be fighting like this," said the thin man's wife.

"Well, we are," said the thin man.

The sound of rifles firing became fainter. The thin man picked up a can of beer and drank from it. The dim flashes and rumbling sounds of bombs and artillery shells exploding in the far distance continued.

"Imagine taking the beer I didn't finish," said the thin man.

"Honey, let's go downstairs now. The air conditioning will be so nice," said the thin man's wife.

The thin man and the thin man's wife walked towards the doorway.

"Good evening to you, Mr. and Mrs. Franklin. It has been very pleasant to speak with you tonight," said the Japanese man.

"I might be referee. Good night," said the short man.

"Good night, Mr. Shoda, Mr. Wylie," said the thin man's wife.

"Good night," said the thin man.

"Honey, are you sure you don't remember if I was wearing the green beads at dinner?" said the thin man's wife.

"I don't remember. I don't think so," said the thin man.

"They're probably on the credenza," said the thin man's wife.

FOURTEEN

AT THE RANCH

The President fed the pigs. The President fed swill to the pigs. The President poured swill into the feeding trough of the pigs. "I reckon the Prime Minister's going to shack up here this evening," the President said to the visitor. The President looked at the pigs at the feeding trough. The pigs scrambled at the feeding trough. The President smiled. "Sure are greedy muckers, ain't they? I said to the Prime Minister, 'Sir, you all had best get your tail down here right quick.' "

The President was happy to be in the country. The President was happy to be away from the capital and at his ranch in the country. The President did not know why he could not always live in the country at his ranch. "I sure as hell can run this country just as good right from this here place," the President said to the visitor. "I got every goddamn thing I need to do it with right here, too." The President pointed at telephone wires and radio transmitting towers near the ranch house. The President pointed at helicopters in a cattle pasture. "You all see that there little man yonder feeding hisself grits?" said the President. The President pointed at a short bald man sitting at a lawn table. "That there's the Secretary of State."

The President poured swill into the feeding trough of the pigs. "Yessir, I reckon I could do just about anything I took a notion to right from this here spot," the President said to the visitor. "Suppose for instance this minute I was to go stark raving loco and took a notion into my head to wipe out the entire civilized universe. You all watch this now." The President blew a pea whistle. A pea whistle hung on a cord around the

President's neck. *A man carrying a briefcase quickly stepped from behind a barn. The man wore a military uniform. The briefcase was locked to the man's wrist.* "This here fellow is the one who's got all the top secret call names and authentications and codes and such so I can wipe out the Bolsheviks over the radio," *said the President.* "How about you all showing this gentleman here the message I'd put on the radio just now to wipe out the Bolsheviks." *The man carrying the briefcase looked at his watch and at the documents in the briefcase. He wrote out a message. He showed the message to the visitor.* "Ain't that just something? I wouldn't have to move my ass a plug foot," *said the President. The man carrying the briefcase said he supposed the message was not to be dispatched.* "Don't you all be dumb, son," *said the President.* "There ain't hardly no reason this morning to wipe out the entire civilized universe." *The man carrying the briefcase shrugged his shoulders uncertainly.*

The President poured swill into the feeding trough of the pigs. The President looked at a pig. The pig squealed. The pig rooted at the President's shoe. The President frowned. The President kicked the pig. "Sure is a noisy bugger, ain't it?" *said the President.*

BACK AT THE RANCH

He chased after deer. He chased after deer riding in the car. He chased after deer in the deer park of the ranch. He chased after deer riding in the white Continental convertible. Reporters riding in other cars followed him chasing after dear in the deer park.

He walked in the yard of the ranch house. He wore a beige ranch suit. He wore a yellow shirt. He wore a Stetson hat. He carried a rifle. Reporters walked with him in the yard of the ranch house. A gopher was on the lawn of the ranch house. He aimed his rifle at the gopher on the lawn of the ranch house. He shot at the gopher with his rifle. He missed the gopher. "Dammit," he said.

He liked being at the ranch. Reporters asked him if he liked being at the ranch. He liked being at the ranch more than being at the capital. He had always liked being at the ranch more than being at the capital. Now he would spend a lot of time at the ranch. Reporters asked him if now he would spend a lot of time at the ranch. Reporters asked him if there would be many changes made at the ranch. There would not be many changes made at the ranch. He pointed at a landing strip. He would continue to use the landing strip. He pointed at a helicopter. He would continue to use the helicopter. He pointed at a hangar and a radio transmitting tower. He would continue to use the hangar and the radio transmitting tower. He pointed at bodyguards. He would continue to have twenty-six bodyguards. He pointed at wildflowers. He would continue to enjoy the wildflowers. There were wildflowers on the ranch. The wildflowers on the ranch had been planted. The wildflowers on the ranch had been planted by members of the Air Force.

He would not miss his old office in the capital. Reporters asked him if he would miss his old office in the capital. He liked his new office in the city. He had a new office in the city. There was teak paneling in his new office. There was bullet-proof glass in his new office. There was a helicopter landing pad on the roof of his new office. His new office was a copy of one of his old offices in the capital. There were three television sets in his new office. There was a galley next to his new office. There was a button on the desk in his new office. He could push the button on the desk in his new office. He could push the button on the desk of his new office whenever he wanted a bottle of soft drink. His staff had new offices. His staff had twenty new offices. There was a room full of his papers. Photographs of him were in the room. There were two hundred and fifty thousand photographs of him in the room. There was air-conditioning in his new office. The air-conditioning in his new office was powerful.

"Yes, sir," he said. "Right there on top of my desk I could pretty near freeze oranges."

He sat on the porch of the ranch house. Reporters sat with him on the porch of the ranch house. A black man served the reporters lemonade and cookies. He would not miss being out of office. Reporters asked him if he would miss being out of office. He liked being out of office. He liked being at the ranch rather than at the capital. He liked not having the responsibility of the office. He liked not having to make decisions. He liked not having to decide every day what decisions to make. He liked not having to decide every day what decisions to make before his nap. He liked not being followed by the man carrying the bag. "Comes a day and they call the roll off and your name ain't on it," he said. He liked not having his name on the roll. He felt good not having his name on the roll.

He was pleased with what he had accomplished. Reporters asked him if he was pleased with what he had accomplished. He had achieved many accomplishments. He had achieved many important accomplishments. He had made many important new laws. The best thing had been to make the new laws. He had done the best thing and made the new laws. He was proud to have made the new laws. He was very proud to have made one of the new laws.

"That there law is like the Emancipation Proclamation except it goes beyond the states in rebellion," he said.

He would not have made any decisions differently. Reporters asked him if he would have made any decisions differently. It had been difficult to make the decisions he had made. It had been difficult to make the decisions he had made but he had made them. It had been difficult to make the decisions but he had been right to make them. It had been difficult to make the decisions but it had been necessary to make them. He had suffered for making the decisions he had made. He would not have made any decisions differently although he had suffered for making them. Sometimes it was necessary to suffer for making the right decisions. Certain persons had the opinion he should have made the decisions differently. He was not angry with them. He respected them. He respected their opinions. They had not had to make the decisions. He had had to make the decisions. He had had to decide what were the right decisions. He had made the right decisions. He would not have made any decisions differently because he had made the right decisions.

"Mama said to me, now you all be sure of doing the right thing, son," he said. "And I reckon that's just about what I done."

He said there would be peace in the world. He said there would soon be peace in the world. Reporters asked him if there would soon be peace in the world. There would soon be a peace treaty at the peace conference. He had made it possible for there to be a peace treaty at the peace conference. He had had to make sacrifices to make it possible for there to be a peace treaty at the peace conference but he had made them. Sometimes it was necessary to make sacrifices. His greatest aim had been to achieve peace in the world. Sometimes it was impossible to achieve one's greatest aim. He had not achieved his greatest aim but it had been impossible to achieve it.

"It kind of snuck away from me," he said.

A gopher was on the lawn of the ranch house. Sitting on the porch of the ranch house he aimed his rifle at the gopher on the lawn of the ranch house. He shot at the gopher with the rifle. He missed the gopher.

Reporters asked him if he had any hard feelings against any members of the press. He did not have any hard feelings against any members of the press. The members of the press had had their job to do. The members of the press had done their job to the best of their ability. He had had his job to do. He had done his job to the best of his ability. There was always a certain strain with the members of the press. There had been a certain strain with the members of the press. The strain with the members of the press had not been great. The strain with the members of the press had been very small. He had had good personal relations with all the members of the press. He was glad the strain with the members of the press had been very small. He was glad he had had good personal relations with all the members of the press. He had many good friends who were members of the press. He was glad he had many good friends who were members of the press.

"All you newspaper fellows are real fine folks. Matter of fact there's one of you all had a grandpappy was with my grandpappy at the Alamo," he said.

He did not have any grudges. Reporters asked him if he had any grudges. He had never had any grudges. He had never had any grudges against anyone. He was full of gratitude. He was full of gratitude for everyone. Reporters asked him if he did not have any grudges against the men who had attacked him. He did not have any grudges against the men who had attacked him. He would miss his friends. He would miss the men who had attacked him. He had not retired because of the men who had attacked him. He had retired for the good of the country. He had made a sacrifice for the good of the country. Sometimes it was necessary to make a sacrifice for the good of the country. He respected the men who had attacked him. He respected the opinions of the men who had attacked him. Everyone had his opinion. He had his opinion. Other men had their opinions. Sometimes men's opinions were different. There was no reason for men with different opinions to have grudges.

"This minute there ain't a bad feeling for anybody in my heart," he said.

A reporter asked him if he had argued with his subordinates at the end of his term in office. A reporter had heard it said that he had argued with his subordinates at the end of his term in office.

"That ain't nothing but a damned lie," he said.

The reporter said he understood that he had argued with one of his subordinates at the end of his term in office. The reporter understood that he had argued with one of his subordinates about the naming of a baseball stadium. The reporter understood that he had argued with a subordinate when the subordinate had named a baseball stadium for one of his political enemies.

"Now don't you all go repeating lies like that to me, boy. I don't take kindly to folks who do that. You ought to of learnt that by now. Maybe you're forgetting I'm just a private citizen now who just might get an idea in his head to tell you all to get off my property and get the hell out of here," he said.

A gopher was on the lawn of the ranch house. Sitting on the porch of the ranch house he aimed his rifle at the gopher on the lawn of the ranch house. He shot at the gopher with his rifle. He hit the gopher.

"Hah. Smack dead in the belly button," he said.

ABOUT THE AUTHOR

Painting by Marcia Flammonde

John Wirth is a retired typist. He worked in Syracuse. Syracuse was the typewriter capital of the world. He claims to be gay.